KISMET AND KISSES

UNEXPECTED ROMANCE ANTHOLOGY

WRITETEAM

INEXHAUSTIBLE MEDIA

Kismet and Kisses

Unexpected Romance Anthology

Written by CoffeeQuills, Sylvain St-Pierre, Catrina Taylor

Copyright 2024

Cover by InExhaustible Media

978-1-63310-056-5

978-1-63310-057-2

InExhaustible Media

Thomasboro, Il

10 9 8 7 6 5 4 3 2 1

CONTENTS

CELESTIAL BONDS

A FIGHT ON THE FRINGE STORY - CATRINA TAYLOR

K aia's fingers danced across the glowing navigation panel as she deftly adjusted the ship's course, tweaking the thrusters to perfectly line up their approach to the space station.

Her simulator score flashed, indicating a near perfect docking sequence. She allowed herself a brief smile of satisfaction before resetting the controls. No time to dwell on success when stellar piloting required constant dedication and practice.

This protoplanet station was her current home, but Kaia's ambitions stretched far beyond its orbit. Someday she would navigate the furthest reaches of the galaxy as an elite cosmic explorer. For now, she still had much to learn. The navigation simulator awaited her next input.

With a deep breath, she began the approach sequence again.

This station served as both a manufacturing site for starships and a training academy for pilots, mechanics, and other industry specific positions.

Kaia was one of the top navigator trainees, determined to join the ranks of expert navigators who guided massive starships through the cosmos.

She spent her days immersed in studies - poring over complex star charts, memorizing hyperspace lanes, and practicing navigation simulations. The mental demands were intense, but Kaia had a gift for spatial awareness and trajectory calculations.

While she repeated routine movements, her mind wandered to her family back home. Kaia felt pressure from her family to settle down. They struggled to understand why she'd want to be around a violent, emerging planet learning to fly instead of on the farm with them. Her parents and siblings loved her dearly, but struggled to comprehend her thirst for exploration over a stable life planetside. Kaia dreamed of exploring the cosmos, encountering new peoples, visiting unheard of worlds, and enjoying every new adventure. For now, she remained focused on her training, pushing aside any doubts or distractions.

Having mastered the simulator, Kaia was eager for the final stage in her training - hands-on flight experience. But first, an unexpected requirement: one hundred hours of maintenance work alongside a starship mechanic before any navigator could graduate.

Though initially chafing at being taken off the simulator, Kaia soon saw the wisdom in this bonding time with an actual ship. As her fingers got grimy, replacing worn engine parts, she gained insight into the inner workings of her vessel.

She raced out of the simulator and out the door.

Kaia hurried down the corridor, nearly skidding as she arrived at the hangar bay. She was late meeting Lucas to work on the SX-Orion per the mechanic training requirement. Glancing around, she spotted Lucas underneath the freighter's engine housing, tools in hand.

"You're late," he commented, not unkindly. "Simulator run long?"

"Yeah, sorry," Kaia said. "I lost track of time practicing."

Lucas slid out from the engine compartment. Kaia appraised him properly for the first time - messy dark hair, intelligent eyes, the soft blue of his skin shone beneath the grease smudge on one cheek. His expression held no judgment, only patience.

"No worries," he said. "I know how the thrill of piloting grabs you. But part of being a great navigator is understanding your ship. Let's get you started on the intake manifold repair."

Kaia nodded, chastened but grateful for Lucas's calm demeanor. As much as she loved the simulator, duty to her ship and training came first.

Once she repaired the ship, it would be hers. She could fly it home and visit her family. She could also surf the stellar waves from one planet to the next, encountering people and cultures she only dreamed of.

Lucas slid under the outdated Salinian light hauler shuttle, flashlight in hand. His instructor, Mechanic Telo, wanted him to evaluate the engine design for inefficiencies. This aging ship would be a good test case.

"Remember, look at energy flow as well as the physical parts," Telo said above him. "Find where power gets lost."

Lucas nodded, tracing the snaking fuel lines and generator connections. He loved this type of meticulous analysis, optimizing systems like a complex puzzle.

Near the engine core, Lucas noticed a web of tangled wires and conduits. "Here's an excessive knot of power routing. Introduces resistance."

"Sharp eyes," Telo said. "Suggest a solution."

Lucas visualized reconfiguring the layout. "Consolidate and straighten the most essential lines. Remove non-critical duplication."

"Excellent. Always improve efficiency," Telo nodded. "Now, how would you lead a student to identify that wiring knot?"

Lucas considered his teaching approach. "I'd have them start by tracing individual connections to understand the system's logic. Once they map the overall flow, tangled areas become obvious."

"Yes, sound methodology," Telo agreed. "And what if they struggle to see it?"

"Then I'd visualize it together from the beginning," Lucas said. "Repeated hands-on walkthroughs until the anatomy is intuitive."

Telo smiled. "Patience and persistence. You will mentor well."

They moved to the propulsion systems next. Lucas' face lit up, examining the intricate thrust controls, possibilities swirling.

"With some modifications, we could improve maneuverability here," Lucas suggested eagerly. "Adjusting these vernier thrusters to articulate independently could really amplify agility." He outlined the approach, demonstrating his solution's impact.

Telo eyed him thoughtfully, then said, "Have you considered pursuing the Engineering degree? You have the right innovative mindset."

Lucas rubbed his neck. "I never thought that far beyond Mechanics certification."

"Perhaps you should," Telo replied. "The stars need that creative vision of yours."

A few days passed and he was back at it again.

Lucas slid back under the SX-Orion's engine housing, deftly tightening connections on the intake manifold. Piloting held little allure for him, but the mechanics of flight - now that fascinated him endlessly. Since childhood, Lucas found solace in the orderly logic of engines and machine systems. Ships spoke to him in a language of compressed air, electromagnets, and warped metal, which he intuitively understood.

Now a senior mechanic trainee, Lucas bore his responsibilities seriously. Every change in the flight design, or adjustment to a ship's schematics, inspired him to learn more. Every ship was like a fun new maze to explore. There was nothing like the sound of a working engine lifting off the platform and humming as it moved out to space, knowing he made it possible.

Teaching wasn't his favorite part of training, but he understood the reason for it. His parents were professors. He was more hands-on than academic. They always taught him that if he really knew something well, he'd be able to teach someone else. When the school program assigned him to a navigating trainee, it made sense to him. Unfortunately, Kaia was his third trainee.

The dean booted his first navigator from the program because they dipped out of the mechanic training part of their course so often it was pointless to be enrolled. The second dropped a crush on the professor and that turned into a mess during training.

Thankfully, their problems weren't held against Lucas as a trainer. Unfortunately, both set him back months from graduation. While the school sought to pair him with a reliable navigator, he pushed forward in other aspects of his program.

Being able to teach a fellow student how to do the things he does was the last test he has to pass.

When Kaia was assigned to him, Lucas feared she'd do what the others did. Half interest in fixing any part would lead to vehicles falling apart mid flight. Kaia showed up with a wrench in hand on the first day of training. That set an entirely different tone.

Lucas knew he'd finally finish this part of his training.

With Kaia, he held no frustration over her simulator-induced tardiness. He recognized in her the same all-consuming passion he felt for repairing and improving these vessels. Just as diving into an engine's inner workings enthralled him for hours, the thrill of piloting grabbed Kaia and didn't let go.

Lucas' patience stemmed from this deep understanding.

For this shy, gentle-hearted mechanic, the greatest joy lay not in flying among the stars, but in providing the means for others to sail those cosmic seas. In time, dedicated navigators come to appreciate the hours spent delving into the SX-Orion's systems.

Working with a navigator meant he learned to improve on designs and create better options for pilots. Live feedback from those testing the improvements ensured he could repair and enhance the vehicles more effectively.

After several hours repairing the intake manifold, Lucas slid out from under the ship and began packing his tools.

"That should do it for today's repairs," he said. "You're a quick study. You picked up manifold calibration faster than anyone I've trained before."

Kaia smiled at the praise. "I'll admit, I'm seeing how hands-on experience can enhance my navigation abilities. Understanding how all the systems interconnect helps visualize the whole ship."

Lucas nodded. "Exactly. When navigating through tricky conditions, knowing your ship's quirks and limits is invaluable." He closed the tool kit and stood up. "For example, with the way this model's fuel lines run, intense lateral thruster burns can cause temporary surges. Nothing dangerous, but good to keep in mind."

"Interesting, I'll have to account for that on sharp course changes," Kaia replied with appreciation in her voice.

As they left the hangar, Lucas added, "I know you're eager to get flying for real. We'll have you space worthy in no time."

Devastation

Kaia smiled. With this patient student mentor showing her the ropes, she hoped to graduate soon. Her family's expectations seemed distant now. She was exactly where she wanted to be - on the path to navigating the stars.

She stretched out on the bed, staring at the projection of the local stellar system on the ceiling. She imagined various paths and speeds from one side to the other. It took very little to get lost in this sort of thinking. Hours spent thinking about the many trips she'll be taking soon lull her to sleep.

Kaia's communicator beeped with an incoming call from her mother. She answered with her usual cheerful greeting, expecting one of their regular catch-up conversations. Unfortunately, her mother's worried face quickly shattered that expectation.

"Kaia, I have difficult news. Jaren is ill - it's nyliactic fever. The doctors," Mom took a deep breath and then continued, "they don't think he'll recover. You need to come home right away, before it's too late."

Nyliactic fever was rare and often fatal if not treated immediately.

Kaia reeled in shock at the news. Jaren had always been the picture of health. Her big brother looked out for her growing up. They were the best of friends, getting into and out of childhood mischief together.

When Kaia expressed dreams of becoming a pilot, Jaren was her biggest supporter, spending hours with her in flight simulators.

Guilt twisted Kaia's stomach - she should go see him. Her studies and training, until now, occupied all her focus, leaving little time for staying in touch. It had been days since they last caught up. He seemed to be a little sick, but nothing problematic or life threatening.

"I know your training is important," her mother continued, "but family comes first. Jaren needs you now, however long he has left. I already sent a formal withdrawal request to the academy."

Kaia felt her dream of flying the stars retreating - *how could she focus on that now?* Leaving everything behind would deeply hurt. Her bond with Jaren ran to the core of who she was. Her big brother needed her.

For now, her future among the stars could wait. It had to wait. More important things required her attention.

The next day, Kaia went through the motions of preparation, her usual eager energy evaporated. She dragged herself to the hangar to meet Lucas, unable to muster her typical cheerful smile.

As they began their work inspecting the navigation computer, Kaia struggled to retain what he was teaching.

"Everything okay?" he asked. "You seem off today."

Kaia sighed, weighing how much to share. Lucas had become a trusted friend these past weeks. "I got some bad news from home," she began hesitantly. "My brother is really sick."

Lucas set down his tools, giving her his full attention. "I'm so sorry to hear about your brother. It's a tough time for things to happen, with graduation so close. I take it you're close with him?"

"Very close," Kaia said sadly. "I'll be withdrawing."

Lucas nodded, but his eyes showed concern. "Withdrawing may not be your only choice," he said gently. "Perhaps a leave of absence or remote learning could allow you to finish."

Kaia huffed. "How could I remotely learn how to repair the SX-Orion?"

Lucas pondered for a moment. "We could schedule remote conversations to review everything. I could record detailed videos of the repair processes. You could access them remotely and practice on a mechanic's simulator. " He shrugged. "We do it all the time in the first year of training."

Kaia blinked in surprise. Disappointment was replaced by an inkling of hope. Her focus had been on getting home to Jaren. She couldn't see a way around withdrawing, but Lucas offered one. This option might not force her to give up her dreams.

For a moment, she relaxed.

"Thank you," she said warmly. "Your suggestion means the world to me. If you have time later, would you come with me when I meet with the director? I'm not sure how that simulator works, and having an expert with me would be a big help."

Lucas nodded. "Of course. We'll figure this out together." He smirked. "I can't lose my best student."

She chuckled. "Best, or only?"

He shrugged. "Either way, we are in this together."

The Meeting

Director S'ara T'Nos had decades of experience training cadets, both as a former navigator and ship captain. Director T'Nos reviewed Kaia's withdrawal notice, their pastel green Doesi skin crinkled as the letter continued. When Kaia and Lucas entered, S'ara came around the desk to grasp Kaia's hands in the traditional Doesi gesture of warmth.

"I am deeply sorry to hear about your brother's illness," S'ara said. "But perhaps total withdrawal from the academy is unnecessary. There are alternatives we can explore."

S'ara guided Kaia to sit, while Lucas took a chair beside her. The director's tone was kind but firm. "Kaia, you are one of our most promising navigator trainees. Your test scores and simulations are exemplary. It would be a great loss to give up on your dreams so close to graduation. Do you want to withdraw, Kaia?"

"No, ma'am." Kaia shook her head sadly. "I don't want to withdraw completely. But my family needs me right now."

S'ara templed their fingers thoughtfully. "Let's find a path that balances both. For instance, remote learning could allow you to complete academic courses from home. The practical training presents more of a challenge, but not insurmountably. Perhaps a delayed graduation would be in order."

"My academic courses are complete. I have two sections left." Kaia took a deep breath and let it out slowly. "Repair and live flying."

Lucas leaned forward eagerly. "If I may, Director - back in the hangar, I proposed recording comprehensive mechanic training videos for Kaia. She could access them remotely and practice repairs using a simulator."

"An excellent notion," S'ara declared. They turned back to Kaia. "Well? Is that an approach you feel comfortable with?"

Kaia nodded, straightening her shoulders. "Yes, I believe so. The simulated mechanic training, combined with a delayed graduation, would allow me to spend critical time with family without withdrawing from the academy." A smile crept across her features.

S'ara returned the smile warmly. "Very good. We are in agreement. We will formalize a plan for remote and delayed completion over the next year. I know you will qualify for graduation, even on this adjusted timeline."

"I know I will too. Once the mechanical training is done, the only other class I need is practical application. Flight School." Kaia exhaled in palpable relief. With her friend's support and director's guidance, she could go home without losing everything she'd accomplished until now. "Someday I will be among the stars," Kaia declared with fresh determination in her voice.

S'ara squeezed her shoulder gently. "You have the heart of a true navigator. We will ensure you reach the heights you are destined for."

"Thank you, Director T'Nos," Kaia said earnestly, "for understanding my situation and helping find a way forward."

Lucas added his sincere thanks as well. The two trainees stood, with Kaia feeling as if someone had lifted a weight from her shoulders. There was hope.

"I will complete the details of your remote and delayed completion plan," S'ara assured them. "For now, spend this week tying up loose ends. And Kaia - be with your family. We will be here upon your return."

Kaia and Lucas exited the office. Her mind swirled with all that needed to be done before her departure. Despite the challenges ahead, there was a sense of optimism.

Preparation

Over the next week, Lucas worked closely with Kaia to wrap up her hands-on training before departure. He would miss her bright spirit around the hangar, but focused on getting her prepared.

Lucas walked Kaia through specialized maintenance routines for deep space travel. "You'll want to watch the oxygen scrubbers," he instructed. "On longer voyages, they need recalibration every month."

Kaia carefully noted each step, asking sharp questions. She came so far from the simulator-obsessed trainee he first met. Her keen desire to learn bubbled over through everything they did together.

While tuning the navigation computer, Kaia's enthusiasm became contagious. "These new holographic charts are incredible! I can't wait to really put them to use."

Lucas chuckled. "You'll have the entire galaxy mapped before long."

Lucas realized he would sorely miss their camaraderie - Kaia felt like a kindred spirit.

As they calibrated the computer, their banter flowed easily. Their friendship had truly become the highlight of his time in training. He started wondering what graduation would be like if she weren't there. He didn't like that thought at all.

They both worked hard to pursue their passions. On her final day, he focused on getting Kaia ready for the journey ahead.

Lucas showed Kaia how to access the mechanic training videos he recorded. "It's not quite the same as in-person," he admitted, "but should help you practice remote repairs."

Kaia gave his hand a warm squeeze. "You've gone above and beyond as a mentor." She met his eyes. "I'll miss working together every day."

"As will I, but I'll be making you a video every day like if we were working together. Then when you get back, they can test you for the next round."

Kaia smiled warmly. "I don't know how I'd still be in class without you. Thank you."

"I'm happy to do it. It's a great option for us both. I don't graduate without a great student." Lucas smiled as he stood.

Over the next few days, his mind wandered back to what Teaching Mechanic Telo suggested about seeking a degree instead of a certification. With his first successful student being forced to change paths and schedules, it might be the right opportunity for him.

At Home

Kaia powered up the mechanic simulator after dinner, ready for her regular lesson from Lucas. Right on schedule, his call came through. She worked through the recorded video earlier in the day. Her evenings were spent going over things she didn't master on the simulator. When his soft blue smile appeared on the screen, she felt connected to her training again.

"Let's run through the intake valve adjustments again," his miniature hologram figure said, smiling.

Kaia smiled back, feeling her stress melt away. She followed Lucas's virtual demonstrations, growing more confident with the repairs.

Afterwards, they chatted about how her family was holding up and life around the station. Kaia realized she looked forward to these calls each day, beyond the mechanic practice. Just talking with Lucas soothed her soul. The realization surprised her. She didn't set out to make friends, but finding one along the way was a nice bonus.

"I appreciate you taking the time for these lessons," she said. "It makes everything feel less distant."

"Of course," Lucas replied. "We'll have you spaceworthy in no time. But I'm happy to lend an ear too, as a friend."

Signing off each night left Kaia already looking ahead to their next call. With Lucas's support, she was determined to aid her family and complete her training.

It was reassuring she remained on track for her goals.

Lucas Remotely

Lucas ended another mechanic training call with Kaia, feeling fulfilled. Through their remote sessions, her expertise in maintaining and repairing ships grew daily. At this rate, she would ace the hands-on evaluations.

Yet Lucas grappled with his own impending graduation. As a student mechanic, he needed to prove mastery by teaching another. Guiding Kaia through repairs on her ship allowed him to complete that requirement. He would wait for her to return to take her test before he would graduate.

Getting another student could move this effort forward and he could graduate soon, but Kaia was working hard. He'd have to leave before she returned if he did that. It didn't feel right. Accepting the later graduation gave him the opportunity for the engineering degree and he'd be there for Kaia too.

Bringing this proposal to Director S'ara in the morning made sense. There would be opportunities to work while at the academy and with some support, he might even get a smaller shuttle to work on for variety too.

Besides, Kaia deserved friendly support when she came back to transit the gauntlet of evaluations. He could get her ship ready for when she's finished testing. Serving as Kaia's mechanic a while longer benefited them both.

At their next video call, Lucas demonstrated proper thruster calibration. Kaia grasped the concepts quickly, though missed hands-on practice. Their rapport flowed naturally as Lucas instructed her on upkeep and repairs.

"You're making great progress," he praised. "We'll have your ship space-worthy in no time, and that will make testing much easier. I think they even picked out the SX-Orion you'll be repairing when you're here. I saw them moving one out of the main hangar after all the others finished testing."

"Wow. That really makes this feel real." She took a deep breath. "You think I'm ready?"

"Yeah. You are. Your ship is ready too. All the work you would have put into your ship has been honed and completed. Once you've finished testing on mechanics, you're going to be ready for live flying."

Privately, Lucas looked forward to more collaborative lessons. Teaching Kaia the intricacies of mechanics gave him purpose. When she returned to the simulator and hangar, he would be there to meet her.

Jaren's Loss

Kaia sat down for her usual mechanic lesson with Lucas, feeling drained. Jaren's health had taken a concerning turn, disrupting sleep and occupying her thoughts.

When Lucas's image appeared, his smile shifted to concern. "Is everything okay?"

Kaia sighed heavily. "Jaren's condition has taken a bad turn. The doctors are doing what they can, but his prognosis is declining rapidly." She trailed off, eyes glistening.

Lucas nodded somberly. "I'm so very sorry to hear that. Please, take all the time you need. Tell me how I can help, if I can help."

Kaia explained how Jaren continued to worsen despite treatments. She spent every free moment at his side, but nothing seemed to help. Her parents worked tirelessly to cover his mounting medical costs, but it didn't look promising.

"I feel so powerless," Kaia whispered. "He's always been my closest confidante, and now I can only watch him slip away." Tears spilled down her cheeks.

Lucas took a deep breath. "You're doing everything possible for Jaren. I know these are just words, but please don't blame yourself. Fate deals us each a different hand."

Kaia wiped her eyes, managing a shaky smile. "It helps more than you know to talk this through with someone. Although fate isn't something I put faith in. It's heartbreaking we're dealing with this. My family is so focused on Jaren, they can't see past the heartbreak."

She went on to describe happy memories with her brother over the years - climbing trees as kids, stargazing and dreaming together. Lucas listened intently, interjecting occasionally, but actively listening. She didn't even realize how badly she needed to be free enough to talk about all of this.

After almost an hour, Kaia's shoulders straightened slightly. "I didn't mean to unload everything on you today."

Lucas shook his head. "You never need to apologize for opening up. I'll always be here to listen." He hesitated before adding delicately, "If you ever need a break from the pain, even for just an hour, I'm only a call away."

Kaia's eyes softened with gratitude. "Just hearing your voice helps tremendously. You have a beautiful gift, Lucas."

With time and care, her inner light would shine again.

Lucas took a bracing breath as Kaia's call came through, knowing she brought tragic news. Her beautiful face was etched with sorrow.

"Jaren passed this morning," she whispered. Lucas' heart shattered for his dear friend. He wished so badly to embrace her.

"Kaia, I'm so very sorry," he said gently. "Jaren was a remarkable soul. Please let me know if there's anything at all I can do for you and your family."

They spoke at length about Jaren - sharing tears, both sad and joyful. Lucas tried to provide comfort, giving Kaia room to express her heartache.

When the call ended, emotions roiled within Lucas' heart. Needing distraction, he went to the hangar where Kaia's ship waited. Losing himself in maintenance tasks brought some small sense of control instead of helplessness.

Days dripped by while Lucas waited for another call from Kaia. He didn't want to intrude on her mourning period, but he ached waiting for her. Days became a week, then two. Each day, he continued to work on the ship. Each moment that inched by, he adjusted the SX-Orion to further improve it. He wanted it to run as close to the simulator as possible.

When his additional courses were approved, Director S'ara told him he could continue as a paid employee while finishing his advanced course work. The class he needed to finish from the standard classes was the one Kaia was a part of. As a mechanic working for the academy now, he knew he had access to anything he needed for repairs, updates, or empowerment of the other students he worked with. This kept him busy.

After two more excruciating weeks, Lucas finally worked up the courage to call Kaia. "I'm so sorry to disturb you," he started hesitantly. "I just wanted to check in as a friend. But if now isn't a good time, don't worry."

Despite the heavy sadness in her eyes, Kaia gave a small smile. "It's alright. I suppose it's time I rejoin life." She sighed. "I was just helping my parents prepare. We're all struggling. I know must return soon."

Lucas nodded somberly. "I understand, and I'm still here for you. We all grieve in our own way. Don't rush yourself." He hoped he brought some comfort.

They talked long into the night, Lucas drawing Kaia gently back out of her shell. Though the light in her eyes remained dimmed, he had faith it would reignite in time. At one point, he even saw the glimmer of a hint of a smile.

For now, he would walk with her through the darkness, a friend for as long as needed.

A Return to Training

Kaia stirred awake as the shuttle approached the training station orbiting the protoplanet she looked forward to waking to again. Rubbing her eyes, she gazed out the window at the familiar sight she'd missed.

Trepidation rose within Kaia. Her mind drifted to her brother and family. She ached at the idea no one would be home with her parents now that Jaren was gone. Yet a small ember of hope flickered, too. Soon she would be with Lucas again, his gentle soul a balm for her own.

Her thoughts drifted to Lucas, conjuring his kind features. She thought about the way his eyes crinkled when he smiled reassuringly. The warmth and compassion in his voice during their training calls that seemed to embrace her even from afar. The way blue anywhere often brought thoughts of him to the forefront of her mind again.

As the station grew closer, other heartwarming memories of their friendship surfaced. His infinite patience guiding her through repairs one step at a time. The genuine joy he took in her mechanical improvements. It really inspired her and reminded her of the better things ahead during the darkest period.

Lucas became her rock through it all.

Their time apart revealed the true depth of their bond. With him by her side, she just might successfully traverse this difficult road back to the stars. Her future awaited, shadowed by loss but brightened by possibility. This emotion she wanted to dwell in.

The shuttle docked with a hiss, ramp extending. Kaia stepped out, breathing deeply the familiar recycled air. Director S'ara waited, their pastel skin crinkling in a smile.

"Welcome back, Kaia. We've missed you around here." Director S'ara T'Nos embraced her warmly.

Test Prep

Over the next few weeks, Kaia spent every free minute preparing to prove her proficiency repairing the SX-Orion. Lucas quizzed her daily, patiently reviewing anything she struggled with.

"You've got this," he assured her. "Just take it step by step. Don't push yourself. You can always come back to a repair if you can do another."

The day of the evaluation arrived. Kaia walked to the SX-Orion hangar, Lucas by her side. She recited engine parts and procedures in her head, visualizing the many hours spent practicing. The examiner gave her a series of tasks - replace the air filters, calibrate the thrusters, realign the plasma injectors.

Kaia took a steadying breath and got to work.

First, she removed the primary air filters, coated in a fine layer of space dust, and replaced them with clean units. Kaia then moved to the lateral thrusters. Mentally consulting Lucas's lessons, she calibrated the pressure valves and realigned the twin ion engines.

Next came the plasma injectors. Kaia crawled under the engine housing, scrutinizing each injector nozzle. Three had fallen out of sync, compromising ignition sequencing. Using a phase calibrator, she realigned their pulse frequencies. It took her longer than when she was training, but she needed to make sure it was perfect.

After testing a fuel purge system for leaks and replacing a cracked compressor belt, Kaia stepped back. Her coveralls were smeared with grease from the long overhaul.

Finally, Kaia looked over everything again, wiping her grimy hands on her overalls as she moved.

The evaluator, an expert mechanic with decades of experience both working on the vehicles and teaching others, approached the repaired vessel. With only three tasks, her results have to be perfect.

She rocked on her feet. Lucas settled against a wall not far away. Despite his long, blonde hair falling in his eyes, he seemed unphased. She folded her hands and unfolded her hands.

Graduation Celebration

The examiner hunched over the exposed engine, checking each plasma injector's synchronization. Kaia fidgeted nervously until Lucas gave her a look she knew meant things were fine. Not a single crease formed on his blue skin. His face remained relaxed. She didn't know how he could do that when his graduation rested on her results.

The examiner reviewed her thruster calibrations, confirming the pressure valves were properly tuned. Kaia bit her lip, watching him test the air filters, review the thrusters, and fuel purge system. She reminded herself that Lucas's thorough lessons prepared her for this.

Finally, the examiner switched on the engine. It hummed perfectly, with no leaks or issues. He monitored it for several minutes, double-checking Kaia's compressor belt replacement and meticulously examining every part she had touched.

Shutting the engine down, he finally turned to Kaia. Her heart pounded in her ears. He continued to input data on the tablet he held. She wiped her hands on her overalls again.

After a few more minutes of silence, the examiner broke into a smile and said, "Well done, Navigator. You clearly have mastery over this ship's mechanical operations. Congratulations on passing the evaluation with flying colors."

Kaia exhaled in relief, barely hearing his praise over the rush of joy. She turned to Lucas, embracing him tightly. A moment later, she quickly released him and stepped back. Still bouncing on her toes while the examiner shook Lucas's hand, she could hardly hear him explain, "And congratulations to you as well, Lucas. Kaia's outstanding performance is a testament to your skilled teaching. It's obvious you understand what we need to keep a ship in space."

After the examiner left, Kaia turned to Lucas excitedly. "We should celebrate! I finally get to move on to flight training and you'll be graduating soon."

Lucas smiled. "Agreed. This calls for a festive night out. What did you have in mind?"

"Dinner at that new zero-g restaurant?" Kaia suggested. "We can feast while floating weightless to mark our accomplishments."

"I love it!" Lucas replied. "We'll toast your upcoming flights and my graduation in high style."

Lucas smoothed his shirt, taking a steadying breath. He hadn't been this nervous for a dinner since his first academy dance years ago. Waiting outside Kaia's quarters, he reminded himself this was just a friendly celebration between trainees.

The door slid open and Lucas' mouth went dry. Kaia looked radiant in a shimmering dress, reddish hair laying in perfect zero-g waves around her smiling face.

"You look very sharp," Kaia said, eyes bright. She took his arm and Lucas felt electricity course through him.

"As do you. You're going to outshine every star in the sky," he replied. Kaia laughed musically as they headed to the restaurant.

Tomorrow he would graduate, and Kaia would begin flight training. Tonight felt full of possibility.

As they walked, Kaia chatted eagerly about finally piloting an actual ship soon. Her enthusiasm stirred feelings Lucas didn't dare examine too closely. In what felt like moments, the pair arrived outside the Zero restaurant.

Lucas gazed around the futuristic restaurant interior as they floated through the entry tube. Patrons drifted from room to room, propelling themselves gently off the velvet walls.

Their server led Lucas and Kaia to a cozy chamber. In the center, a table was bolted halfway up the wall, settings secured by magnetic plates. Their server gestured to a menu screen embedded in the wall. Lucas and Kaia made their selections by touching the desired dishes.

A vast viewport revealed the star-speckled expanse outside.

"What an amazing place!" Kaia exclaimed, adjusting easily to the weightlessness. "Though I hope I don't get space sick."

Lucas chuckled. "Just keep your eyes on the stars, not your stomach. This will be a meal to remember."

They anchored themselves by the table to take in the glorious expanse outside the viewport. Lucas felt humbled, yet uplifted by the glittering display. Beside him, Kaia sighed contentedly. Something about her smile felt brighter against the stars, or maybe it was this moment. Graduation was finally happening. His family would arrive before the ceremony and his best friend glowed at the promise of finally getting to the stars. It couldn't be more perfect.

When the server arrived with their food, they placed it in the covered place settings. Lucas marveled at the novelty of dining weightless. With Kaia here, the night felt magical.

Their server popped the lids off the anchored dishes with a flourish. Lucas found himself face to face with a floating medley of colorful cuisine.

Kaia effortlessly plucked a purple sphere from the air and plopped it in her mouth. "Mmm, this nebula soup is stellar!" She grabbed floating utensils, maneuvering gracefully.

Lucas grabbed his magnetic fork, stabbing at a cube of cosmic beef. It evaded his grasp, bumping his nose.

Kaia giggled, catching the cube. "Here, watch me." She demonstrated dipping the cube in sauce before bringing it easily to her mouth. Kaia effortlessly plucked a purple sphere from the air and placed it in her mouth. Her delighted expression was contagious.

He stabbed at a different cube of cosmic beef, but it bumped his cheek this time, escaping his grasp. Kaia giggled and caught it. She placed it in his mouth, and his gaze lingered for a moment longer than intended.

Lucas tried again, this time successfully. "Thanks, I'm still adjusting to eating without gravity." He sipped his starberry juice, trying not to spill.

"You're getting the hang of it!" Kaia encouraged, as she easily devoured a meteor muffin. She looked utterly in her element, while Lucas fumbled to keep food contained.

As they continued their meal, Lucas improved, though not matching Kaia's natural ease. When his asteroid cake went drifting by, she nabbed it and fed him a bite playfully. Lucas hoped his blue skin concealed any blushing.

Between tasty morsels, conversation flowed comfortably about training adventures and mishaps. Kaia described her excitement about flight training while Lucas shared funny mishaps from his mechanic lessons. Laughter filled their private cosmic vista, as they enjoyed the novelty.

As the last crumbs cleared, Kaia bit her lower lip thoughtfully. "We should probably start heading back. You'll want to get rested up before your family arrives for graduation tomorrow."

Lucas tried to conceal his disappointment. "You're right, of course."

Kaia squeezed his hand. "We have to come back here to celebrate in a year when I graduate too."

Lucas brightened. "I look forward to that immensely."

They drifted back through the tubes. Once they were back on the gravity deck, they walked back to the residential section together.

At her quarters, Kaia pulled him into an embrace. "Thank you for an incredible evening," she whispered.

Despite not wanting to let go, he lingered only a little longer than a friendly hug before responding, "It was the perfect graduation celebration."

Before anything else could be shared, he left. As Lucas headed back alone, her smile lingered in his mind. Just one more day until he was a certified mechanic. Yet now, more than ever, he looked ahead to Kaia's graduation.

Graduation Ceremony

Kaia entered the small, intimate ceremony hall. She folded her hands together while looking for a place to stand. Sunlight streamed through viewports overlooking the protoplanet below. Clustered before a simple stage, Lucas's proud family turned to smile at Kaia as she slid into the crowd.

On stage, Director T'Nos was concluding their remarks, praising Lucas's achievements. "...and so it is with great pride that we honor Lucas Ronan today for his exceptional talents and diligence. His brilliance and skill have overwhelmed the faculty."

Lucas stood nearby, wearing his new graduation uniform, eyes modestly downcast. The uniform hugged his form, accentuating his muscular arms.

Kaia could see his shoulders bouncing gently with suppressed excitement and pride.

As the director finished the speech extolling Lucas's accomplishments, Kaia felt honored to be present for this special moment, launching her dear friend toward a bright future. She stood eagerly, ready to celebrate with him.

"And so, it is with great honor that I call Lucas Ronan to the stage," announced Director S'ara T'Nos.

Lucas walked up, back straight, and stood before the director.

"For your outstanding achievement in engineering, I hereby award you this degree in Mechanical Engineering," said Director T'Nos as she handed him an engraved plaque, symbolic of his hard work and achievement even far beyond the certification he initially sought.

Lucas's face broke into a wide, proud grin as his family and Kaia erupted into raucous applause.

The director raised a hand for quiet and continued, "In recognition of your skills, we are also offering you a full-time engineering role here at the academy training facilities. We would be privileged to have you."

Lucas's eyes widened in surprise. "I accept, and thank you for this opportunity," he said sincerely, shaking the director's hand.

Kaia's heart swelled with joy for her friend. His brilliance was finally being rewarded.

At the reception, Lucas was surrounded by smiling well-wishers eager to congratulate the accomplished graduate. Kaia hung back happily, letting his family smother him with praise.

His mother soon broke away and surprised Kaia with an embrace. "Thank you dear, for being such a motivation to our Lucas," she said, eyes glistening with pride. "He speaks so highly of your shared work."

Kaia smiled warmly. "The honor was mine. Lucas is an exceptional mentor and engineer. His degree is well deserved."

Lucas came over and introduced Kaia to his father, who shook her hand heartily. "We're so proud of Lucas! An advanced degree already, and that job offer - the galaxy is his oyster!"

Her mind briefly lingered on Lucas's smile, and how at dinner the night before it made her heart beat harder, even in zero gravity.

Mingling with his ecstatic family, Lucas often snuck glances across the room at Kaia, as if to confirm she was still there. Each glimpse sent her stomach into somersaults. When Lucas returned to Kaia's side, she squeezed his arm. "All your hard work and patience pays off. This is only the start for you."

"Having you here means everything," Lucas replied, eyes bright.

Kaia's was overcome by joy being a part of this moment with Lucas.

As the reception ended, Lucas lingered even as his family prepared to leave. He turned back to Kaia, scuffing his foot awkwardly. "I guess this is goodnight for now?"

Kaia tucked her hair back, nodding reluctantly. "I do need to head to flight registration..."

"Lucas! Come on, we're supposed to meet Dad!" his brother called impatiently.

"Just a minute!" Lucas said over his shoulder. He rocked on his heels uncertainly. "Well, I should probably..." Lucas paused, before asking, "We'll talk soon?"

"Yes, very soon!" Kaia promised.

"Well, I suppose I should..." He rocked on his heels, stuffing his hands in his pockets.

"And I do need to register for those flight classes..." Kaia said, willing time to slow. Of course, it didn't.

Another lingering moment of silence between them and Lucas looked over his shoulder at his brother before he said, "Goodnight, Kaia" and kissed her forehead. Then it seemed as if he put on antigravity boots and floated away faster than she could respond.

After the shock of his kiss passed, Kaia's shoulders sank as she watched him go. The ghost of his embrace from their dinner still clung to her.

His Future

Lucas awoke feeling optimistic excitement about the day ahead. The morning sun streamed through his window as he stretched happily. Graduation day already felt like a whirlwind.

He smiled, remembering the pride on his family's faces as he accepted his engineering degree. All their support over the years meant so much. Lucas looked forward to seeing them off later today before they headed home. Mostly, he looked forward to making plans to actually make it home soon, now that school was no longer his priority.

His thoughts lingered on moments from the past few days. The fascinating zero-g dinner with Kaia, floating and laughing together. Her radiant smile at the ceremony that made his heart skip. That lingering goodbye neither wanted to end. He didn't know when something changed, but it had. His friend felt like more to him. Something about Kaia's enthusiasm for her passion, dedication to her family, and drive to always be at her best inspired him in a way he couldn't explain.

Checking his messages, Lucas grinned, seeing Kaia's invitation to join her first flight in the SX-Orion today. He swiftly accepted. By her side in the cockpit was exactly where he wanted to be. He swiftly responded he would be there.

After replying to Kaia, Lucas hurried to meet his brother in the station rec room they had reserved for handball. As he entered, his brother raised an eyebrow. He was quick to respond, "What?"

"You seem extra chipper this morning," his brother commented, tossing him the ball. "That graduation success still sinking in?"

Lucas bounced the ball absently. "Yeah, just feeling really optimistic this morning."

His brother nodded. "Engineering degree, fancy job offer - I'd say your prospects look bright."

They volleyed the ball back and forth. After a few hits, his brother added casually, "Of course, doesn't hurt that Kaia is so cute and clearly into you."

Lucas fumbled, his flush giving him away. "What? No, we're just friends," he insisted weakly.

His brother laughed. "Uh, huh. Friends who can't stop making eyes at each other." He raised an eyebrow. "She is human, you know."

Lucas busied himself with the ball. "I hadn't really noticed."

"Oh, come on," his brother pressed. "I saw how you two were at the ceremony yesterday."

Lucas scoffed, making a sharp return. "You're imagining things. We're just good friends."

"Oh, come on," his brother pressed with a grin. "I can't blame you for falling for a pretty human like her."

"It's not like that," Lucas muttered, willing his blush to fade. His brother's words rang more true than he cared to admit.

They volleyed faster, Lucas chasing awkward saves as his flush deepened. His brother was reading him like a star chart.

"Come on, just admit she's gotten to you," his brother teased, lobbing the ball out of reach.

"You're imagining things," Lucas muttered, retrieving it.

His brother held up his hands, grinning. "Hey, no judgment! I'm just saying you two clearly have a connection."

Lucas scoffed, but the ball dribbled off his paddle. His brother's accuracy was unnerving.

"Uh oh, your face is turning awfully blue," his brother laughed. "She's really got you flustered, huh?"

Lucas stammered meaningless denials, pulse hammering. He didn't know if his pulse raced because of the game, or because of the conversation.

His brother clapped his back sympathetically. "It's okay to have feelings, Lucas. The question is - what's holding you back from pursuing them?" his brother asked, lobbing the ball.

Lucas returned it, contemplating. "Well, I did just start a new job here..."

His brother spiked a tricky shot. "You were trainees together, though."

"True..." Lucas aimed at a sharp cross-shot.

They rallied swiftly, words punctuated by the ball's impacts. After several hard volleys, his brother asked casually, "It's not because she's human, is it?"

Lucas nearly fumbled his return. "No, not at all!" He added spin to regain control.

His brother nodded. "Didn't think so." The ball bounced rapidly between them. "Besides, mom and dad would be really disappointed if that's all that held you back."

"It's more..." Lucas jumped, narrowly saving a spike. "Now I'm an engineer here, while she's still a student."

His brother remained silent.

Lucas backpedaled, brow furrowed. "Fraternizing probably goes against protocol." He lunged, paddle connecting sharply.

His brother swooped low for a dizzying save. "Your positions don't have to be an obstacle, though. It's not like you're her teacher. You're in different departments now."

Lucas darted left, keeping the rally alive. "You really think so?"

"Absolutely." His brother rolled the ball across his shoulders before sending it sailing.

They exchanged several more hard volleys. Then Lucas's brother reared back and spiked the ball hard cross-court. It hit the floor before Lucas could reach it.

"That's game!" his brother declared. He clasped Lucas's shoulder. "Best two out of three next time?"

Lucas grinned, catching his breath. "You're on."

His brother glanced at his watch. "We should hit the showers. Don't want to miss Mom and Dad's shuttle departure."

Lucas nodded, sobering. "Right, of course." He set down his paddle. "And... thank you, for the talk. You've given me a lot to think about."

"Anytime." His brother smiled warmly. "Follow your heart. The rest will unfold how it should."

They headed to the lockers, Lucas feeling reflective.

Her Future

Kaia settled into the pilot seat of the SX-Orion, preparing for preflight checks. Before initiating startup, an encrypted call flashed across the console. She answered hesitantly.

"Hello Kaia Kent," a disguised voice carried over the coms.

Kaia tensed. "Who is this? How are you accessing my ship?"

"I represent parties interested in your potential. We've monitored your progress closely."

Kaia began looking around the ship for unexpected speakers or cameras. "Why me? I'm still in training," Kaia countered.

"You have natural skills beyond your peers," the voice said calmly. "With the right opportunities, you could excel faster than the academy allows."

Kaia hesitated, intrigued but wary. "What kind of opportunities?"

"A chance to pilot experimental ships on the fringe, make first contact with new civilizations, be a pioneer on the galactic stage," the operative described.

Kaia's pulse quickened at the thought. "And if I refuse?"

"No repercussions," the voice assured. "We only seek willing partners. Consider carefully before graduating limits your options."

Kaia chewed her lip. "This is a lot to process..."

"Naturally," the operative said. "For now, focus on your test flight. We will be in touch soon."

The call blinked out, leaving Kaia conflicted.

This was the moment she had trained endlessly for - her first official solo flight. She inhaled deeply, centering her surging emotions. Time to focus. The skies, er, stars, were waiting.

Running through the startup sequence, Kaia's hands glided expertly across the controls. She smiled as each system blinked online - navigation, propulsion, life support. Like a concert pianist, her fingers danced across the console executing the memorized steps.

"SX-Orion, this is Flight Control, do you copy?" The voice crackled through her headset.

Kaia toggled the transmitter. "Flight Control, this is SX-Orion, I copy. Preflight sequence is nearly complete."

"Copy SX-Orion," Control responded. "You are cleared for departure in T-minus 5 minutes."

"Affirmative Control, I am ready for departure." Kaia could barely contain her eagerness. She triple-checked fuel levels, energy reserves, and cabin seals. All optimal.

As launch grew imminent, euphoria threatened to bubble over. Kaia took a centering breath. Patience. She prepared endlessly for this moment. Gazing out the viewport at the vast expanse of stars, she whispered, "I'm coming for you soon."

Settling back into her seat, she gripped the thruster controls firmly. In mere minutes, her dreams of flight would finally take form. Kaia smiled serenely, feeling completely in her element.

A sudden knock on the hull startled her from her focus. Peering out the viewport, she saw Lucas waving sheepishly. Kaia laughed and hit the switch to lower the gangplank, gesturing him aboard. "Glad you could make it!"

Within moments, Lucas joined her in the cockpit. "Sorry for the last minute arrival," he said, strapping into the copilot seat. "I wouldn't miss this for anything."

Kaia grinned excitedly as they quickly re-verified all systems. Lucas kept the mood light with jokes about bringing motion sickness meds. The easy banter relaxed Kaia as the launch approached.

Just then, the transmission cracked. "SX-Orion, Flight Control. You are cleared for departure in T-minus 60 seconds."

Kaia toggled back. "Copy that Control. SX-Orion ready for departure." She exhaled slowly, hands caressing the thruster controls. This was it.

She exchanged an exhilarated smile with Lucas. Kaia could already feel the freedom of the open stars calling.

"SX-Orion, you are cleared for takeoff," came the command.

"Copy that, Control." Kaia eased the thrusters forward, gently lifting them off the deck. She angled them out towards open space, the station shrinking behind.

"Course laid in for a standard orbit," she reported over the headset.

"Looking good SX-Orion. Enjoy your flight," Control responded.

Kaia grinned at Lucas as they glided smoothly into the darkness. "So, how was your family's visit? Are they safely back home now?"

"Yep, seen off this morning after much farewell fuss," Lucas chuckled. "It was great having everyone here to celebrate graduation."

Kaia smiled. "You must be proud - and that new engineering job!" Her hands moved along the controls as she added, "You looked good in your uniform yesterday," Kaia said. She felt her cheeks flush and busied herself adjusting their trajectory.

Lucas smiled appreciatively. "How does the SX-Orion handle for you so far?"

"Like a dream!" Kaia laughed. She fired stabilizing thrusters, curving them around the glowing planet. No simulation compared to this exhilaration. She tapped the transmitter. "Control, SX-Orion has achieved standard orbit."

"Copy that SX-Orion, looking great," Control affirmed.

Kaia leaned back with a contented sigh, stars streaming past the viewport. She was finally here, doing what she was born to - flying.

They chatted casually as Kaia monitored systems and corrected their course where needed. The SX-Orion handled like a dream.

Lucas smiled. "Any nerves up here?"

"Not a bit!" Kaia assured, readjusting their angle. She was completely at home guiding them smoothly through the cosmos. Kaia laughed, patting the console. "I can't believe this is finally real." She adjusted their trajectory, the planet rolling beneath them. "Though not as unbelievable as you earning an engineering degree. I thought you were going for a mechanics certificate?"

Lucas rubbed his neck humbly. "Oh, that. Well, I had some time before my favorite student returned to test her repair skills. So I figured why not?"

Kaia grinned. "Such modesty. But really, that's impressive."

"Only because of excellent motivation," Lucas replied, with a lingering gaze at her, instead of the planet.

Kaia felt her cheeks warm again and quickly checked instrument levels. "Regardless, you should be very proud."

"I'm proud of us both," Lucas said. "We make a pretty great team, star pilot."

"That we do, star engineer," Kaia smiled, savoring the musical tone their titles took on.

"Star engineer and star pilot," Lucas mused. "Has a nice ring to it."

Kaia smiled. "Hard to believe graduation was just yesterday. That zero-g dinner feels so long ago now."

"Right? Crazy how much has happened," Lucas agreed. He rubbed his neck. "But uh, that was a really nice evening together."

She bit her lower lip. "Oh yes, I enjoyed it a lot too!" Kaia said, feeling her cheeks flush as she checked instrument panels.

"It was just...really great getting to spend time together outside of training," Lucas continued. "Conversations seemed to flow so easily and comfortably."

Kaia nodded, heart quickening at the fondness in his tone. "It was wonderful." She met his eyes, feeling suddenly shy. "The food was delicious."

"So was the company." Lucas's eyes darted away from Kaia.

Kaia opened her mouth to say something, but then flight control reached out. "SX-Orion, Control. You are cleared to return to the station. Make one full orbit around the station before the landing sequence."

"Copy that," Kaia responded, shaking herself alert. She banked toward the approaching station, thoughts still lingering on their dinner. "Entering orbit now," Kaia confirmed, thoughts swirling as she banked around the station.

Completing the loop, she switched on automated landing protocols. "SX-Orion beginning arrival sequence."

"Copy, looking good," came the reply.

The shuttle moved into the landing sequence on autopilot as the station loomed large in the viewport. The incredible view felt larger than she expected. In awe of the completed flight, feeling excited and overwhelmed all at once she turned to Lucas, ready to say something.

He was already facing her, eyes glimmering. Lucas gazed at her intently, hesitantly, as though seeing her truly for the first time. Her throat went dry. She forgot what she wanted to say to him. Lucas brought his hand up to gently cup her cheek.

When their lips finally met, a feather-soft caress, it felt like the most natural thing after flying.

As they pulled back she softly asked, "Now what?"

Lucas smiled. "Whatever we want."

JACKAL AND KROSEPH

SYLVAIN ST-PIERRE

P^{art-1}

"To loot!" Jackal raised his tankard and, with a laugh, the two girls seated across from him clanked theirs against it. The two guys pressed against the fighter held on through the motion, their hands pressed against his muscled chest over the rags that still pass for his shirt.

The two hadn't been on the run with him, Jenny, and Linia. Jackal had noticed them on their walk back, and when he'd pulled each against him with promises of fun times, they'd eagerly remained.

Jackal wanted fun after the harrowing experience this run had been. He wanted to forget the skittering of rats and the screams of his team's sorcerer and rogue, as they stumbled and vanished behind the boulders and were swarmed. He'd seen what the rats had done to the lean man since he'd reached him in time to keep the dungeon from dissolving the body and equipment.

Jackal had thought himself immune to death after the years in the pits and dealing with his father's goons as they tried to drag him back home.

Seeing the body as he took the amulet had made him realize that every death he'd seen and caused before had been clean; they'd been dead, and that had been the end of it. This body had been mutilated by the rats and that image was—

"Can we go?" the man on his left whispered, his hand moving lower and groping.

Jackal down what was left of his ale to swallow the moan, then kissed him hard.

"Soon."

He kissed the other guy. He was the more corpulent of the two, so he wouldn't be left out. And he made a face afterward at the taste. Jackal laughed. not everyone was used to drinking ale. Some people were used to finer things. He had to have been one. He'd have to get used to it now that he was here. Jackal didn't see there being anything more expensive than ale, considering the meager coins they left the dungeon with.

Jackal was going to help him get used to it, because Jackal needed to forget the run. And the best thing for that was ale and guys.

"Server!" Jackal yelled over the others in the inn. "More ale!"

The inn was the only alternative to the food tent, and the porridge there, passing itself off as something edible. So anyone with coins, mainly the workers building up this place, filled the large room. Jackal hadn't gotten enough coins from handing back the amulet, armor, and rogue's knife, for them to enjoy food, but ale was cheap.

The server, a boy near his age with messy black hair and the tan of someone who has spent more time in the sun than any server Jackal had ever met, and brown eyes that glinted with amusement replaced the tankards.

"Who has the copper?" he asked, holding the tray against his body, the loose shirt ballooning at the motion. Jackal offered it, only to pull it away as the server reached, forcing him to put a hand on the table to keep from losing his balance.

"How about you join us?" Jackal asked. "I still have plenty of energy to satisfy you along with these two?"

The server chuckled. "I have to work." He deftly snatch the coin out of the fighter's hand, but Jackal grabbed his arm before he pulled away.

"Come on, have some fun with us. I'll make it worth your while."

"you have two strapping boys to keep you busy."

"but it'd be more fun with you, I can tell."

The server looked at him, then at the other two. He bit his lower lip, then opened his mouth.

"Kroseph!" a guy yelled over the crowd. "Stop making out with whatever guy you're charming and get back to serving. You don't want Dad to send you back home, do you?"

"I told you," Kroseph said in what to Jackal looked like an attempt at hiding disappointment. "I have to work."

Jackal let go of him and leaned to watch the server's backside vanished in the crowd.

"If you aren't happy with how we're doing our jobs, Russ!" the server yelled back. "You're welcome to get out of the kitchen and help us serve."

Jackal grabbed a tankard and raised it. "To guys!"

"I'll happily drink to that," Jenny replied, clanking tankards. "To men who know how to please me."

"You so aren't at the right table," Linia laughed.

"You never know." Jackal looked from the guy nibbling on his shoulder, looking back at him with lust to the one who'd unlaced Jackal's trouser and had a hand in them. "one of these busy guys might know a thing or two about pleasuring girls. if they can still move once I'm done with them, I'll tell them where to find you."

"I can find my own men," Jenny replied with a bark of laughter. "Your tastes in guys leaves something to be desired."

"What are you talking about?" Jackal protested. "I desire everything about guys."

"And you'll take any who throw themselves at you," she countered, eyeing the one who made Jackal grunt with a less than amused expression.

"They didn't throw themselves at me," Jackal replied once he had his voice again. "I pulled them to me, told them how hard we were going to fu--"

"And they are next to you after that kind of invitation makes it clear they aren't for me." She smirked over her tankard. "Please keep them."

"Good." the fighter grinned. "Now I don't have to worry about making sure they can walk once I'm out of the bed." He finished his ale in one long swallow, then stood, grabbing his trousers an instant before they fell. "I've got them," he told the guy. "How about you pull your hand out and we get back to it, and more where the neighbors aren't going to care how loud we get?"

With a grin to the girls at the table, he headed to the door, pausing when he noticed the server, Kroseph was his name, through a gap in the crowd. Their eyes met and Jackal made a quick motion to the door, but the server shook his head, then vanished.

Part-2

Kroseph stepped out of the door accompanied by the young man who had spent his break in his room with him.

"That was good," the man said and Kroseph smiled.

"It was." It had been good and controlled and heated. Much better than whatever offers that fighter had made him over the last weeks. Wildness was all Jackal was, like the animal he shared the name of. Probably as savage in bed, too.

Kroseph shook himself. He preferred his men quieter.

"If you want to do this again, seek me out." The man waved as he headed for the door.

Maybe, maybe not. Jackal headed for the bar, where his sister Elpida, as well as two of the local guys their father had hired, were putting tankards on their trays.

"Is this ever going to slow down?" his sister asked tiredly.

"Better hope it doesn't," their father said, setting an ale barrel in the empty spot. "investing here wasn't cheap. I don't want your mother to be able to rib me when we go for a visit."

"Then how about you hire another cook," Russel said from the kitchen's door. "If I'd known I'd be stuck always doing it, I'd have stayed home where I can share the duty with six other people."

"You're going to have help the instant I can find someone in this place who can cook. If I'd been able to afford more than just the three of you, I'd have done it."

"You found people to help El and Kro easily enough," Russel said before vanishing back into the kitchen.

"Servers are easy," the father yelled after him, then looked at the two locals at the bar. "Don't mean to imply anyone can do your work, but training you is easier than getting a decent cook."

And with the way one of the new server was eyeing Kroseph, as well as flirting with any patron who so much as smiled at her, there was another way some of them were easy. She'd have to stick to looking in his case. Even if Kroseph were interested in women, he didn't take coworkers to his bed.

"Kroseph." his father lopped a pouch at him. "the order of meat's waiting at the platform. I need you to bring it. Anyone I'd hire is too busy."

"Have you offered them a night in Kro's bed?" Elpida offered. "The way the customers are looking at him, I'm sure they will be willing to put anything else aside for that." She smiled. "That fighter certainly looks strong enough to carry anything, and he's been quite vocal in his interest in my brother."

"No," Kroseph stated. "Not him. Anyone but him." He frowned. "No one. I'll decide who I take to my bed, and for my reasons. Not because Father needed them to do work for him."

"Good," His father said. "I have no intention of turning this inn into the kind of establishment my cousin runs. Now off you go, if there's an ale seller there. Order us twelve casks. The way they're going through the stuff, I'm going to have to make more room among the supplies for them."

The exclamation of pain made Kroseph break into a run.

He was somewhere between the inn and the transportation platform, but unsure how far. With all the work taking place, he'd had to detour and now he was lost and among partially constructed buildings, with the walls high enough to keep him from seeing the eight pillars that marked where the platform was.

"Please stop," the victim pleaded.

"Oh, I will," his aggressor mocked, "once have had my fun with you."

The Runners were about the one thing Kroseph didn't like. They seemed to be nothing more than ruffians at best, and outright criminals at worse. Even Jackal, for all that he never caused trouble at the inn, if Kroseph discounted the times the man nearly ended up naked because of how eager his companies were, had wildness about him that yelled of living on the wrong side of the rules.

Then, there were those adventurers, who were supposed to keep the peace. Kroseph had seen them spend more time watching the Runners fight, a few placing bets, than stopping them from causing trouble.

"No!" the man's voice rose in pitch, and Kroseph pushed harder. He had to bet there before—

"He said to stop," a voice Kroseph recognized said in a tone that wouldn't take flotsam from the aggressor. Surprise caused him to slow.

"How about you mind your own business?"

Kroseph peered around the partially constructed wall. He'd been right, Jackal, that fighter who kept trying to talk him into sharing a bed, even when he already had guys with him, stood between a rougher-looking guy Russel had thrown out of the inn on opening day, and one on the ground with cuts on his face from being punched.

"Harassing a Runner makes this my business." Jackal crossed his arms over his muscular chest.

Kroseph was disappointed the fighter wore a worn jerkin over a mostly intact shirt. The fighter might be loud and in his face, but he was nice to look at. His dirty blond hair was longer than Kroseph preferred, but if not for the man's obsession with food, ale and bedding whatever guy offered themselves, he could look past it. The fighter just didn't seem to be able to take anything seriously.

"Get the fuck out of my way, Jackal. That trick's mine to play with."

"Or what?" Jackal replied, smirking.

The punch that sent the fighter's head snapping to the side was hard enough blood sprayed. Jackal worked his jaw as he looked back at the man, who smiled with proud satisfaction.

"That's...not horrible, as far as punches go." Jackal grinned. "How about I show you the way to make sure the guy who's passing you off never thinks to do it again, Arruh?"

Kroseph barely saw the surprised realization on the other man's face before the punch sent his head reeling, pulling his body along. Jackal grabbed his head, keeping him from falling, and brought it down on his knee, sending it back up. He punched him in the stomach, and the man finally ended on the ground.

Krospeh debated intervening as Jackal stepped toward the downed man. He didn't think he should let him kick him, but they were Runners and if he got between them, he could be the one suffering, and he still had the errand to—

Jackal prodded the man with a foot. "You conscious?"

The man groaned.

"Good. You saw what I did? You see what your mistake was?"

The moan could have been a yes.

"Now, how about you pick yourself up, runoff, and see if one of the instructors will give you a potion to take care of this? You probably don't want to be sent into the dungeon in this shape."

The man crawled away, and only once he was out of sight did Jackal turn to look at the man's target; the *trick* he'd mentioned. Kroseph didn't know what the term meant in this context; even with magic to ensure everyone understood each other. But the leering tone let the server guess what the intentions had been.

And the self-satisfied smile on Jackal told Kroseph that other than the violence that the other man had inflicted, he would milk the situation similarly. He stepped back. At least Jackal would treat him well. It was one thing all the guys who spoke of their times with Jackal said; he was wild, but he treated them well.

Kroseph didn't want to be around for the fighter claiming another guy as—

"You okay?"

The caring and concern in the fighter's voice stopped Kroseph. He had imagined it. The fighter couldn't do concern for others unless it was about their bed-relating abilities.

"Don't worry," Jackal said in that same soft tone, "he ain't coming back."

Kroseph peered around the corner again.

The fighter crouched before the other man. Other than his injuries, he looked ordinary enough. Short brown hair, fair skin the way some of the Runners had. He was slender, but Kroseph knew it meant little when it came to Runners.

"What's you do to end up here?" Jackal asked gently.

"Nothing," was the harsh reply.

"We all did something to end up in a cell. I don't judge," Jackal added, then chuckled. "Trust me, I can't judge."

"I didn't do nothing," the young man insisted. "Men came for Papa. Something about an argument he had. Them being paid to make sure he knew to never do it again. I tried to stop them. One hit me, and I woke in a cell. I was waiting for Papa to come for me when they took us away." He fell silent. "Now Papa won't ever know where I am." he sniffled and Jackal watched him.

"That sucks."

The young man glared at him through the tears.

"No, I mean it. It sucks you got this for trying your help your dad. But you aren't going to do him much good if you let someone like Aaruh treat you the way he did. You a rogue?"

"They put me with the fighters."

"You know anything about fighting?" Jackal asked after a stretching silence. "You can probably get in with the archers if you can handle a bow. How about your letters? You know those? That'd be enough to get you in with the sorcerers."

Another shake of the head.

"Abyss," Jackal whispered. "Okay. How about I help you? You saw how I kicked—well, I didn't get to kick him. This ain't the pits, and that about the only place I think it's okay to kick a man when he's down. But you saw how I beat him, right? I can teach you. Help you survive the dungeon, and if Aaruh ever thinks to touch you how he wanted to, well, I'm going to show you where to kick him to make sure he never wants that close to you again. What 'dya say?"

The guy wiped his eyes and nodded. Jackal offered him a hand, pulled him up, then they were headed away.

Kroseph returned to figuring out how to reach the transportation platform, somewhat perplexed at how he'd seen Jackal act.

Part-3

Jackal grabbed the server as he placed the tankard on the table and pulled him onto his lap. "How about you keep me company?" the fighter said. "I'll share my ale with you."

The older man laughed and kissed Jackal's cheek. "When it's not that busy. The old Walrus is going to have my hide if I'm not serving more than you." he winked. "Unless you're willing to hand over more coins to justify me staying with you."

"I'm a Runner," Jackal replied with a laugh. "The guild barely lets us keep enough coins to drown our sorrows in ale."

"Then it's back to work for me." The man pushed off and disappeared into the crowd of the tavern.

"I'll keep you company for some of that ale," another guy said, draping his arms over Jackal's shoulder, then nibbling his neck. "and some of what you're packing. I hear you're good."

"I'm the best," Jackal boasted. He took a swallow from the tankard and handed it over. "And I've got no problem proving it."

"How about I help you with that?" Jackal took the barrel the serving girl had over her shoulder without waiting for a reply.

"I was managing it," she protested.

He smiled at her. "You don't have to worry about impressing me. I see you and the others work among the ruffians that we are. That's plenty." He lowered his voice. "And I'm not into girls."

"I wasn't trying to impress anyone," she replied as he put the barrel into its place among the others. "I was just doing my job."

"And now it's done, so you can go back to looking for someone to have fun with." He headed to his table where the group of guys we waiting, ignoring her further protest. He was tempted to tell her she was protesting too much. She didn't have to act all proper in this place. This was a lot more like the taverns around the Pits he'd fought in than those in the better neighborhoods of his old city.

The woman let out a shrill of distress, and Jackal was up and across the tavern before the guy who'd been on his lap landed on the floor. He grabbed the man's hand as he raised it, ready to slap her back, much harder than she had, but the barely visible handprint on his cheek.

"How about you don't hit the person serving you your food?" Jackal said.

"Mind your own business. I'm going to show her--"

the man's head hitting the table silenced him.

"I could have handled him," she told Jackal.

"But why should you have to when I'm around? You should be free to serve guys who'll treat you better than this one did."

"Like you?" she mocked.

Jackal laughed. "oh no. you want someone much better than me. only sleazy guys find me interesting."

Jackal smiled as he saw the guy standing next to the ale barrel by the transportation platform. His messy black hair was matted with sweat, probably from many attempts at lifting the barrel.

Finally, he'd be able to impress Kroseph enough to get him to say yes to some fun in bed.

"You're that server from the inn," he called, rubbing his hands eagerly.

"That server from the inn," Kroseph replied with a chuckle. "Why am I not surprised that's how you think of me?"

Jackal looked the man up and down, wishing he wasn't wearing the too-large vest over the shirt. He'd like to see more of Kroseph. He'd like to see all of him without clothing, but he'd settle for the slim chest and arms that had to be hiding under the loose clothing he always wore.

Jackal grinned. "With how many guys I know, I'm not going to remember all the names."

"I supposed that to someone like you, so long as they introduce themselves as "I'm Willing" you're happy."

"Exactly!" He frowned even as he grinned. Kroseph's smirk said he'd missed something. He put that out of his mind in favor of moving forward with his plan. "How about I help you?" He made his biceps bulge. "I wouldn't want you to strain yourself with this when I can help strain you afterward."

The man stared at him uncomprehendingly, and Jackal helped him by glancing at the barrel.

Kroseph looked at it. "Oh. you think I need help with that?"

"You have been panting next to it for a while. Hey, I get it. It probably doesn't look as heavy as it is. You might pull something trying. And if you're going to pull something, it should be part of me."

Kroseph rolled his eyes. "Does anyone fall for it?"

"More like bounce on it."

The server looked at him, and Jackal nodded. He'd soon find out he wasn't exaggerating.

Kroseph gave him a slow look over, and Jackal straightened. He didn't pose, like he would after winning a fight in the pits, but he wanted the man to get a good look at what he was going to experience. The server's sigh was all the confirmation he needed of having won him over.

But before Jackal could reach for the barrel, Kroseph tilted it as he crouched.

"Look," Jackal said. "You don't hurt yourself trying to impress me. I already am interested in taking you to—"

Kroseph straightened, hefting the barrel over his shoulder.

"Sorry," the server said as Jackal stared, "but I can't just stand around here and talk." He started walking, giving no indication the barrel was too heavy. "And as flattering as your interest is, this isn't to impress you."

He was two shops away when it registered that the guy was getting away.

He ran after him, wondering why he was running. Jackal had never chased after a guy in his life. Abyss, it was more about fighting them off so he could have fun with one, two, or three of them at a time.

"But you were already sweaty," Jackal said, matching pace with Kroseph. "Isn't it from trying and failing to pick it up?" no, of course not. Not with the practiced ease with which he held it on his shoulder.

"It's from this being the seventeenth barrel I've been bringing to the inn today. Everyone's still too busy for my father to be able to afford paying workers to bring them."

"I'll do it," Jackal hurried to offer. "And I won't ask for much."

Kroseph rolled his eyes. "You think I'm worth that little?"

"What? no, of course not. Wait, how did you know I mean I'd do it in exchange for you?"

"You are an easy guy to understand, Jackal. Everything you do is about getting food, ale, or a guy. You have money from your runs for the first two." Kroseph grinned. "And even if I took money for it, you couldn't afford me."

"I'd never ask you to spend time in bed with me in exchange for money," Jackal protested. "I offer and you say yes because you want to."

"or I say no."

"Or you say no," Jackal echoed, then added, "And I try again."

"you are incorrigible," Kroseph said with a chuckle.

"I don't have to change when I am already so great."

"Sure, let's go with that."

"Are you sure it's not too heavy?" Jackal asked. "I mean, you're a server, and you aren't massive under that shirt."

"And how do you know what I look like under my shirt?"

"I have a good imagination."

"And you imagine me skinny?"

"No, just normal, like any server. And I have bumped into you."

"I'm well aware."

"The inn's crowded," Jackal gave as his excuse. It was, and it had given him more than one chance to get close to Kroseph, but the server was adept at maneuvering through it. "Also, some of your shirts show a bit of what's under them." Glimpses, more than anything else. Enough to make him want to see more. Run his hands over that chest.

"How did you see me in just my shirt? I have a vest when I'm working." he fixed his gaze on the fighter. "So that when someone spills his drink on me, it doesn't get to my shirt."

"That wasn't on purpose. Graytle shoved me."

"Before or after you realized I was there?"

"After. but I don't see what that's got to..."

"I thought you'd see it."

"I didn't tell him to shove me," Jackal protested. "I'd never waste ale that way." He looked Kroseph over. Maybe it would be more of an investment than a waste if it got him out of his shirt? He could offer to lick him clean afterwa—He shook his head. That was cheating. He would get the see the man out of his shirt, and more, but he'd do it honestly. By getting him to say yes.

"It was when it rained a few weeks ago," Jackal said. "You came out of the kitchen in a shirt."

"I'm surprised you noticed me."

"You're easy to notice."

"I'm easy to notice," Kroseph said in a suspicious tone, "in a busy in? do you spend your time looking for me?"

"No," Jackal protested.

He didn't spend all his time there looking for the server. He enjoyed the ale and the guys who joined him. It was just because he spent so much time there that he knew when the server worked and when he wasn't there.

"Aren't you hot?" he asked, because something about what he'd thought was making him uncomfortable.

"Aren't you cold?"

Jackal looked at the thin shirt he'd taken off his dead teammate, then ripped the sleeves off because they were too tight. The pants he'd gotten on a previous run, thick fabric like what workers wore. "It's not even chilly."

"Where are you from?" Kroseph asked. "This feels like I'm up the mountain during the runs."

"Tartanos," Jackal replied. He wasn't surprised at the lack of recognition. If he'd thought there was a chance Kroseph might know of it, he would have lied. "You?"

"MountainSea."

"And it's warmer than here?"

"Definitely. The wind off the sea is always warm. You have to run up the mountain before it gets cold."

"Are there a lot of them?

"MountainSea is carved out of the mountains on three sides, with the sea on the last one. "

"So they're like city walls?"

The server laughed, and Jackal watched the man's brown eyes light up. Those lips move.

"They're like hundreds of walls on top of one another."

"What are?" Jackal had trouble remembering anything from before that beautiful laugh.

"The mountains." Kroseph eyed him.

Right. Something about running? "Do a lot of people run up the mountain with you?"

"With me?"

"didn't you say that you ran up the mountain when you want to be cold?"

"That isn't what I said. And the Mountain Runs only take place during the festivals."

"Oh, okay." What could he say to make Kroseph laugh again? What had he said that made him laugh? There had to be something. It had sounded so nice, and his face had looked so—

He barely stopped before walking into Kroseph. They were by the door of a building Jackal didn't know.

"If you plan on coming in," the server said, putting a shoulder to the door. "You're going to have to use the front door. This leads to the kitchen and only those if us who work here get to use it."

"I thought you worked at the inn."

"Don't work too hard trying to figure that one out," the server said with a chuckle as the door opened and smells of food blew out. "And my name is--"

"Kroseph," Jackal said.

"I thought you only remember guys named I'm Willing."

"What?" Jackal shook himself.

"How do you know my name?"

"the cook yells it when he needs you to get a plate."

"His name is Russel."

Jackal shrugged, becoming uncomfortable with how Kroseph looked at him.

"And you remembered it from all the other names you casually forget."

"I'd remember anything about you," Jackal said, then felt himself blushed.

"That is good to know." the door closed and Jackal kept staring at it.

Why had he said that? And what had that look Kroseph given him meant?

He shook himself again. How Kroseph made him feel wasn't important. What was, was figuring out what this other place he worked at was.

Jackal walked around the building, then stared at the inn's door in confusion.

He shrugged since he was here already. He might as well eat and drink instead of think.

and Kroseph might be the one to serve him.

Part-4

"You know you can go over," Elpida stated, and Kroseph looked away from Jackal and the four other guys laughing at their table.

"Go where?"

She rolled her eyes. "I've seen you watch them, well, him and whatever guys he's with, Kro. Go, I'm sure he's not going to mind having you join him."

"I can't, I'm working."

"it's one of the rare quiet times. Dad's not going to comment. If things pick up, you can come back to help."

He looked at the table in time to watch Jackal reach across and pull the guy into a deep kiss. It was long and sloppy, and—Kroseph looked away. "look at him, he shouldn't be doing that here. He has no manners. He can't be serious. Why would I want to spend time with him?"

"Because he's different from your usual guys?"

"Different doesn't mean better." He walked away from his sister to attend to the new arrivals, utterly ignoring Jackal as he pulled the guy next to him onto his lap and proceeded to kiss him, too.

The guy had no respect for the other patrons what so ever.

* * * * *

"I hope the food's to your satisfaction," Kroseph said, placing the plate before the merchant's son, and a hand on his shoulder, which he squeezed.

"It's always good. Russel never disappoints."

Kroseph smiled. he'd learned his brother's name. Another point in his favor. Along with being well-behaved and dressed. Unlike a certain someone he wouldn't think about, who was being loud in the corner right now with his... cronies. guys who hung onto that fighter like that deserved no better names.

"Enjoy the food."

The merchant's son patted Kroseph's hand and smiled at him. "I will"

He glared in the fighter's direction in the time it took to reach the bar, then he busied himself with other customers because he wasn't going to think about what that Runner was up to.

When he returned to the merchant's son's table to replace the tankard, the plate was nearly empty.

"Are you in a hurry to return to your shop?" Kroseph asked.

"It depends on what else I might have to do," he replied, gazing into Kroseph's eyes.

"would you be interested in spending time with me? My bedroom is just up the stairs."

"I'd like that. Will it interfere with your work?"

"No, I'm due for a break. Let me tell my sister, and once you're done, we can go."

There, he too could have a good time. Jackal's table was quieter now, but it was because the fighter and the two guys left were making out. Kroseph just didn't have to be so blatant about his good times.

"Kroseph!" His father yelled over the people clamoring for drinks at the bar. "There's one of those Runners in the corner taking a chair and not doing anything with it. He needs to spend money or leave. We're too busy for them to just take a spot."

Kroseph looked in the direction his father pointed, but couldn't see through the crowd. Still, he had a direction. He shouldered his way through until he made it to a Runner, alone in a chair in the corner, looking at the floor.

The first surprise was that people gave him space considering how crowded the floor was; the second was who the Runner was. Kroseph wouldn't have believed the fighter capable of the defeated expression on his face.

He placed a hand on the man's shoulder, and blue eyes glistening with shed tears looked up at him.

"Are you okay?" His father's instructions no longer seemed important.

Jackal shook his head. "Lost someone."

"Someone...special?" Kroseph had trouble believing the fighter had anyone special, but considering how many Runners didn't come back when they went in, they'd have to be.

"Not really." The chucked turned into a pained hiccup. "Don't know why this one hurts so much. He wasn't even that good. They shouldn't have put him with us fighters, but I'd been teaching him. He wasn't learning fast." He swallowed. "nowhere near fast enough."

Kroseph realized he had to mean that Runner Jackal had rescued from that brute Aaruh. That he'd still been training him after these weeks surprised him. He didn't think the fighter could focus on anything for that long a time, except, maybe, trying to convince Kroseph to get into bed with him. And to be affected like this spoke of him having cared beyond what that guy could do for Jackal.

The fighter wiped his eyes as he looked around. "You probably need me to get you." He smirked. "No one wants a dumb fighter like me bringing down the mood."

"Stay here," Kroseph ordered, the decisions instantaneous. He went behind the bar and filled a tankard from the ale barrel.

"They gone?" his father asked.

"You said he could stay if he spent money."

"Runners who have money don't sit in corners alone."

Krospeh took a copper from his vest and placed it on the counter. "He paid for it."

His father took and studied it before leveling his gaze at his son. "Don't spend money on them, Son. Runners aren't--"

"It's not about him or what he won't do, Father. It's about me and what I want to do. I want him to have this tankard, and you said—"

"Go ahead," his father replied, hand up in defeat. "Just don't expect anything back from their ilk."

Kroseph closed the tankard and made his way back to Jackal. he was looking at his feet again, and only looked up when Kroseph offered him the tankard.

"I don't have coins for it."

"Don't worry about that. You look like you can use a drink."

Jackal nodded. "Once I'm done, I'll leave."

Kroseph squeezed his shoulder. "Stay as long as you want. This inn is a place to seek rest from the dungeon's hardship, and you look like you can use that." He turned to leave, but Jackal grabbed his arm.

"Thank you, Kro. I'm sorry I'm an ass to you. I don't mean half the things I say."

Kroseph considered pulling his arm. They were busy, and he'd already taken too much time comforting him. But the earnestness in his eyes...

"Then why do you say them?"

"I... open my mouth and they pour out."

Not even an excuse to justify his actions. Jackal could be an ass, and he accepted he was. Somehow, that was refreshing.

"Have you considered not opening it so often?"

The fighter smiled. "How am I going to convince you to my bed if I don't say anything?"

Kroseph chuckled. As he'd said, he opened his mouth and words poured out. "Not by saying that." He took his arm out. "Enjoy the Ale, Jackal. Stay as long as you need to. I have to get back to work."

The crowd quickly cut him off from the fighter, but he couldn't seem to shake his presence from his mind.

* * * * *

Quiet finally filled the inn, and Kroseph found himself looking at the empty chair in the corner. He didn't know when Jackal left, but he hoped the fighter had done so in better spirits.

"Well, that's a look I haven't seen in a while," Russel commented, wiping his hands.

"What look?" Kroseph asked, looking away from the empty chair.

"That faraway look on your face," Elpida replied. "Mixed with thoughts of someone you'd like to do nice things with."

"The last time I saw you with that," Russel picked up, "was about that fighter from the arena, all sweaty as he posed for the adoring crowd. I'm pretty sure you thought he was doing it just for you."

"I'm surprised you didn't run off to go show him how much you liked the show he put on," Elpida said with a grin.

"I was much too young for what you're implying," Kroseph protested, his face heating up at the memory of exactly how he'd intended on showing that fighter how much he'd appreciated looking at him, and the many attempts at convincing his father to let him attend the arena again. As well as the few times he'd snuck into the arena against his protests to watch him fight.

And the one time he'd done something daring and made his way under the seat to do exactly what his sister implied. and been caught by the arena's guard and returned to his father, and the talking-to he received about proper behavior and the bad influence people like that fighter were.

They're just there to be watched, not approached, his father had told him. *Men like that are nothing but trouble.*

"I don't think this one's going to measure up," Russel said.

"You know which of the Runners he's taking a fancy to?" Elpida asked.

"I haven't taken a fancy to anyone," Kroseph protested.

"Dad talked about some Runner taking a chair," his brother answered. "Even sent Kro to chase him off, but instead our brother bought him an ale."

"You spend money on a Runner?" his sister exclaimed.

"He just had a bad run," Kroseph replied in his defense.

"From what I picked up from the servers who saw him," Russel said. "He's a buff fighter."

"No wonder Kro's all over him," Elpida said with an innocent smile plastered on her face.

"I am not all over him."

"Seems he's here often enough, too," Russel continued. "Always with a bunch of other guys."

"Oh, that one?" She grinned. "The fun one. I thought you didn't like him."

"I don't," Kroseph replied, his face burning.

"Okay, I've never seen him blush that hard," Russel said.

"Look, he's good looking, I can admit that. I mean, it's not like he covers a lot of that massive chest of his most of the time. But he's a child." Who stand up to bullies on behalf of someone weak. "All he cares about is getting guys in his bed, and he doesn't care which one or what he has to do to make it happen." Only, he never pushed when Kroseph told him no, or laughed at his advances. He only tried again later. "And I don't think he could survive having one serious thought." But he wasn't joking when he spoke of that Runner he'd trained and lost. The pain had been there on his face. The regret, the reproach.

"Look. I'm happy he had all those guys hanging on him, because I want nothing of that man."

Except, maybe, take his pain away.

Part-5

"Well, hello there," Jackal greeted the server behind the bar. "You look good. You'd look better in my bed."

"No."

Jackal was taken aback by the brusqueness of the reply. He'd been certain there had been a smile forming there. He opened his mouth to let Kroseph know he'd be back later, but the server spoke first.

"Just stop. Okay? I'm not in the mood."

Jackal almost opened his mouth, but didn't trust what would come out of it. He nodded and headed to the table, where three guys waited for him. He plastered on a smile, while trying to figure out how he'd manage to offend Kroseph so badly and quickly.

"Do it again," the guy leaning against Jackal said, awe in his voice.

"What?" Jackal pulled his gaze away from Kroseph, who was now laughing with Russel and Elpida. That was so different from the look Jackal had received as he'd approached the server to show him what he'd learned. That look had bordered on anger. There had been a lot of those recently, and Jackal still couldn't figure out what he'd done to make him angry. He was the same fun guy as usual.

"Do the thing." The guy smiled and motioned to Jackal's hand. "Do it for me?"

It still took time for Jackal to think away from Kroseph to what the guy meant. "Oh, that thing."

The guy's smile broadened. "Yeah."

Jackal looked around. In part because he wasn't comfortable doing that in the inn, where anyone could be watching, but also to see if Kroseph was looking in his direction. This would be a chance to show him what he'd learned.

The server had his back to him, speaking with his brother and sister.

Hopefully Kroseph would be in a better mood after that and more receptive to the demonstration.

He slowed his breathing and reminded himself this was normal now.

This was something he could do, no matter how odd it felt. The oddity was why he preferred keeping doing this where he couldn't be watched, but he wanted to make this guy happy so they'd do a whole lot more afterward.

He felt inside himself for the rubble there. He didn't know how else to think about it. Since returning from his audience with Earth, there was a little rubble inside him he could push around.

It didn't do much. The instructor had shown what an adventurer with the right training could do with earth essence, but Jackal couldn't imagine how he'd take the little rubble inside him and make his entire body stone, it raise pillars and walls with it. All he could do at this point was...

He pushed the rubble to his arm, down it and spread it over his hand, and earth grew around it.

It looked nothing like the gray stone the instructor had changed to. It didn't even look like his hand anymore. More like he'd dunked it into thick mud and pulled it out.

"What does it feel like?" The guy asked, touching it. Gingerly at first, then grabbing and poking.

"It feels like..." he searched for words. "Dirt." He was no good with words

"It's hard," the guy said, pressing down on it.

Jackal barely felt it. He could tell he where on his hand the guy touched, just like if the dirt wasn't there, but he didn't get much of the rest.

He'd slammed a stone on his hand as hard as he could as soon as the instructor had let them go after explaining the basics of his element, and there had been no pain, barely the feeling of the impact. Just the sensation of the stone on his hand.

"Can you use it to make any other parts hard?" The guys asked, reaching under the table to grope the part that interested him.

Jackal laughed. "I don't need the element's help to get that hard." He smirked. "as you can feel right--"

"Let me go," Kroseph ordered, and Jackal was up, the guy forgotten. that had not been the tone of someone being playful. The server was at one of the few occupied tables, one of the three men seated there holding him by the arm. Jackal didn't know them, so they weren't Runners; too old too. Some of the workers then.

"How about you do your job?" the man holding Kroseph said with a smirk, "And service me?"

"That's not the kind of service we offer here," Kroseph offered in a firm tone. "If you don't, let go of me right now. There will be consequences."

Jackal headed for them before Kroseph's bluff could be called.

"And what are they going to be?" the man asked, leering. "get your handler to—"

The man's head hit the table hard enough Jackal stopped in his tracks a few steps away from the altercation.

Kroseph held the man's face pressed in the table, blood pooling around the crushed nose. "You're still holding me," the server said. "Do I have to grind your face through the table to make you let go?" He looked at the other two. "Please don't get involved. I'd hate to have to bar you from the inn for this guy's stupidity."

They shook their heads and drank.

The man whimpered against the table and let go.

"There. That wasn't so hard, was it?" Kroseph released him. "Now. DO I have to consider evicting you, or will you behave properly toward everyone in the inn?"

"I'll behave," the man replied meekly.

"I'm sorry to press," Kroseph said, "but how are you going to behave?" by the tone he had heard that said more than once only to have it acted upon in a different way than what it implied. Jackal loved doing just that when the occasion presented itself.

"I'll behave nicely," the man said in the same meek tone.

"Thank you." Kroseph took the tankard. "I'll be back with your refill and something for you to wipe the blood off your face." He turned and seemed surprised to find Jackal there. "Hello."

"Hi." At least Kroseph was smiling. Jackal kept his mouth shut, looking at the man with the hand over his nose.

Kroseph looked over his shoulder. "You were hoping to save me, weren't you? Maybe that I'd be so grateful I'd take you to my bed?"

Had he even thought that far ahead? He'd been more worried Kroseph would get hurt trying to stand up to that man. "Well, yeah." He was pretty sure Kroseph would have said no, but Jackal wouldn't have let that keep him from trying.

Kroseph patted his cheek. "I'm sorry. I'm not some helpless runner who needs rescuing."

"Do you..." Jackal swallowed. Kroseph had told him no at every turn. If he couldn't impress him by keeping from getting hurt... "need anything?"

Something passed behind the server's eyes, but Jackal had no idea what it was. It wasn't amusement. He'd seen that look often directed at him by Kroseph; not anger, either.

"Yes," Kroseph said softly "but--"

"What is it?" Jackal asked, hopeful for any chance to impress him. "I'll get it for you."

The sigh was filled with disappointment. "No, I don't think you can. Maybe you should go take care of your cr—friend."

Friend? Jackal wasn't here with any friends. Unless Kroseph meant—no, he wouldn't be walking away if he meant he was the friend he'd referred to.

Turning to return to his ale, he saw the guy there, looking at him with hunger in his eyes. That was a look Jackal read easily. And one he had no problem acting on.

Except. He looked at Kroseph. He'd said it clearly this time. No amusement, no lashing out that came with regret that the words. He just didn't need anything from Jackal.

He'd tried everything he could think of, and Kroseph wasn't interested.

That... he swallowed and forced a smile. That wasn't something he wanted to think about right now, and he had someone with a look that said he'd have more fun thing to think about.

"Come on," he told the guy, pulling him to his feet. "How about I show you what I can do with it without the help of earth?"

He glanced over his shoulder as they reached the door. Kroseph was handing a cloth to the man while wiping the blood off the table with the other.

He really didn't need anything Jackal had to offer, did he?

Part-6

"You going to say hi to him, at least?" Elpida asked as Kroseph placed the ale barrel in its spot among the others.

"Who?"

"You know who."

He looked at her. "How about you push too, instead of asking about someone I clearly don't know?"

She rolled her eyes and placed a shoulder against the barrel. "That Runner who's done everything short of ripping the door off the stairs to get to your bed."

"He's already with someone." He didn't have to look. Jackal always had a guy or two with him.

"He's only with someone the way you are with the guys you bring to your bed."

"He's with a lot more of them." The barrel finally slid and settled in place. "At the same time, too." He didn't hold it against the fighter. He was a Runner, and they lived dangerous lives and he celebrated surviving the way he felt like he had to.

"I thought you liked him," she said, wiping her hands with the bar rag.

"I don't dislike him, but—"

"Dislike who?" a familiar voice asked, and Elpida grinned. Kroseph was going to have to think of a way to take his revenge on his sister. He turned. "It'll be how many tankards?"

"Just one."

Surprised, Kroseph looked around the fighter. No one at the tables looked like they were waiting for him to come back. He filled the tankard and took the copper, then turned to head to the kitchen, only to notice Jackal hadn't moved from the bar.

"Is there something else I can help you with?"

The fighter looked uncomfortable. "How... how are you doing? I mean, how is it going?" He motioned around them. "All of this."

"I don't know how the town is doing," he answered cautiously. This was nothing like how the fighter usually talked to him, and he couldn't tell if there was a 'I'm so great you should show me your bed' about to burst out of his lips.

"Not all that, this... place."

"The inn?"

"Yes, the inn. How is it going? You making enough coins? You going to be staying even if there's more taverns opening?"

"The inn's doing well." He smiled. "Are you worried I'm going to leave?"

"No, of course not," he replied so forcefully Kroseph barely contained his laugh. "Anyway. I'm glad the inn's doing well." the fighter took his tankard to a table, and Kroseph eyed the door, expecting guys to come bursting through now that Jackal was seated. When that didn't happen, Kroseph found himself feeling like the sun had turned itself into Claria all of a sudden.

The fighter didn't play games, so what was going on?

Part-7

The hand squeezing his thigh made Jackal look away from Kroseph, who was turning down the persistent advances of another of the patron.

He grinned at the guy looking up at him. "Wanna go have some fun?"

"I was wondering when you'd offer," the guy replied.

Jackal laughed. "If you didn't want to wait, I'm sure some other guy would have been happy to take you to their bed."

"When I want another guy, I'll get some other guy."

"Then let's go." Jackal waved at Kroseph as the server looked in their direction as they left.

Jackal watched Kroseph work.

Not for the first time, he wondered why. The server had made it clear he wasn't interested, and Jackal had run out of things to impress him with. Kroseph was just to...something to be impressed by anything Jackal did.

Too there. was the best way he could think to describe it.

Even Jackal's element didn't seem to impress him. At least Kroseph hadn't asked about his new eye color, the way every other guy who wasn't a Runner had the first time they say his now reddish-brown eyes. His earth eyes.

Kroseph had noticed them, then went on doing what he had as if they didn't matter. As if the fact Jackal now had an element wasn't important. He could do magic, well eventually, and Kroseph didn't seem to care.

All that seemed to matter to him was his work, or guys who worked too much. Jackal had noticed that about the guys the server took upstairs. They were all serious and probably always working when they weren't here.

Could Jackal do that? Get work and always do that? Some of the Runners did. A few were on the construction crews when they weren't on a run.

It was coins, but where was the fun in getting them that way. Jackal liked to have fun while getting his.

He missed the pits.

but if he did it, would Kroseph be interested in him?

Jackal shook himself and finished his ale. He wasn't joining some work crew just to bed a guy. There were easier guys to bed.

"Can I help you?" The woman said. She was muscular, wearing thick cloth shirt and pants, along with heavy looking boots.

"I'm here to train," Jackal replied.

She raised an eyebrow. "You have an element, and I know we haven't gotten anyone new, so how come it's the first time I've seen you here?"

"Didn't think I needed it."

She smirked. "The dungeon's teaching you otherwise?"

"Aren't you afraid it's going to eat you?" Kroseph had asked him with an odd expression.

"Something like that." He didn't know why Kroseph's question had made him think about it. He hadn't cared about the dungeon eating him. It was going to happen, so all he wanted to do was have fun until then.

"Then step forward and show me what you know."

"Jackal." The guy draped himself against the fighter. "Take me to your bed."

Jackal laughed. "Can't do it now. I'm heading for training."

"I'll give you special training." He ran a hand down the front of the fighter's pants.

Jackal chuckled and moved the rubble inside him, split it and pushed them to his arms, spreading it along the way his instructor had showed him. When he picked up the guy, he hardly weight anything.

"I'll find you once I'm down with my training. Trust me on that."

"But I want to have fun now." the guy replied as he was put down. "What happened to you?"

"Nothing." Jackal continued on his way to his training.

Jackal watched Kroseph serve customers from behind the bar. He should go and tell him everything he'd done. How seriously he took his training. It wasn't work, the way other guys the server took to his bed did, but he was a Runner, so it was work still, wasn't it?

He would be impressed, right?

but did it matter?

Jackal had no problem admitting he'd started training because of what Kroseph had said, that look in his eyes. And the thought he'd use that to get the server in his bed had been there too. Still was, evidently.

But at some point Kroseph had stopped being the reason he went. He liked the training. It was nothing like fighting in the pits, and getting his element to do anything was so hard at times he hated it.

But then, when he managed it. He loved seeing the dirt covering his hand thin without softening until he could see his hand again.

If he wasn't doing it for Kroseph, should he be telling him about it?

"There you are," the guy said, dropping into the chair and pressing himself against the fighter. "I expected you to be with the other guys."

Jackal shook his head. "felt like being along and enjoying a drink."

"I can give you plenty to drink in my room," the guy whispered, grinding against Jackal's leg.

Jackal chuckled.

Kroseph stepped out from behind the bar, spoke with customers, exchanged smiles with a guy. The guy nodded to the door and Kroseph shook his head, said something, motioning around them, and the guy nodded.

"Well?" the guy still grinding against him whispered in his ear.

Kroseph didn't need it, Jackal realized. Maybe the server didn't need anything, and that was how he'd been able to turn Jackal down every time.

"I think I'm good," Jackal said.

"Really?" the guy pulled away.

"Yeah." What was it like to take a guy not because of need, but because he wanted to? Not him. Jackal doubted he was the kind of guy Kroseph wanted to take to his bed, but who might Jackal want to take to his. Not because they were offering themself, but because... there had to be some other reason to want that, right?

"are you serious right now?"

"I actually am," Jackal replied, surprised to realize he meant it.

The guy gave him an odd look, then left him to his ale and contemplation.

Part-8

"That's a first," Elpida whispered, and Kroseph glanced at her, then where she'd been looking in time to see the guy who'd been draped against Jackal leave without the fighter.

He looked away before the surprise made him stare. What was going on with him? When was the last time Kroseph had seen the fighter laugh too loudly, make out with guys, try to take someone in to his bed?

Tried to talk Kroseph into it? Was he missing the big dumb fighter saying stupid things, hoping that would convince Kroseph to say yes?

He couldn't be.

Kroseph barely had the time for a nod to his sister as he grabbed the tray holding all the tankards the table needed. The inn was filled again. Runners were celebrating something. He had no idea what, but they had money and they were spending it here. So he had to keep serving them.

"Careful," the man said, taking him by the shoulders and preventing the collision. Kroseph was back on the ground and the guy on his way through the crowd when the red-brown eyes registered, the face, the polite smile and nod before moving on.

Kroseph almost went after Jackal to demand where the suggestive wink had gone to, or the offers for the server to thank him personally later for the help, but a clamor reminded him he had work to do.

he had trouble focusing on that for the rest of the evening, searching the crowd for Jackal so he could demand an explanation.

"Here." The earth covered hand pushed the ale barrel Kroseph had been about to let slip into place, then took the two tankards his sister had placed on the bar and headed back to a table.

Kroseph stared at Jackal's back, too surprised to question what had happened.

"He's younger than his usual guy." Elpida said.

"That's not..." the protest was reflexive, and Kroseph had no idea why he'd been about to defend the fighter against... nothing? It wasn't like his sister was accusing him. But looking at the two, Kroseph didn't get the usual sense around the guys Jackal took to his bed.

Not that there had been a lot of those recently.

"I think he's just another Runner," Kroseph said, then noticed the boy's eyes were a normal brown. "or one of the worker's son. I don't think they—" Jackal noticed him watching, gave a nod and returned to the conversation.

The flick on his forehead had him cursing and glaring at his sister.

"Oh, you're still in there. For a moment there, I thought your mind had dropped into the abyss."

It might as well have, Kroseph thought, since that had to be where the explanation for what was going on with Jackal had to be hidden.

"Tell Russel the meat's real good today."

"wha...?" Kroseph couldn't finish the question as the surprise was simply too much.

Jackal frowned. "I used the right words this time, didn't I?"

"Since when do you know my brother's name? You've never called him anything but the cook."

"You said you didn't like the fact nearly no one used his name."

"I never told you that." no that they'd exchanged more than a few words over the last weeks. Or that he'd been in the inn all that often.

"You told Anietan."

"And she told you?" Jackal remembered the conversation. It had been a long day with a lot of rude workers. If he hadn't told how he felt to another of the servers after yet another one told him to get 'the cook' to change something about the food, he would have done something to the customer.

"No, I was two tables over."

Kroseph stared. "And you heard us?" It had still been busy and loud.

Jackal grumbled something, his tan growing redder.

"I didn't make that out." Kroseph was unusually amused by the fighter's reaction.

"I wasn't watching that hard," Jackal said, looking away.

"But hard enough, you heard us over the noise?" He smiled as the fighter looked flustered.

"I wasn't—I mean, I didn't—" Again, he was mumbling and Jackal fought against laughing.

"Maybe you can pronounce better?"

"You are quite watchable," Jackal said with an exasperated sigh.

"Thank you." Kroseph prepared for what was about to follow and his usual amused—

"Okay." Jackal walked away.

"Wait!" Kroseph called after the fighter, but he only hurried out of the inn, leaving Kroseph wondering what in the abyss was going on with the fighter, and why not bring hit on by him on the rare time they interacted felt so...wrong?

Kroseph approached the table cautiously. The look on the fighter meant there would be no advance, but he also didn't want to chase him off again.

"Is everything okay?" He placed the plate and tankard before Jackal, who looked at it in surprise, then at him. He unhooked the pouch from his belt, but Kroseph placed a hand on his shoulder to stop him. "You've been overpaying with all those single ales you've ordered recently. It covers this." He didn't remove his hand,

"Thanks." He moved the thick slab of meat with his knife. "Lost another one on this run."

"That young one?" Kroseph asked, worried. He'd seen them at the same table a few times. It was definitely not the same as how Jackal had been with the previous guys, but there was something there. A friendship, at least.

"Who, Tibs? No. he's fine. He wasn't with me on this run. Just yet another Runner that fed the dungeon. I barely knew her. Not sure why it's even affecting me anymore."

Kroseph squeezed. "Because you have a heart."

The fighter snorted in his tankard, then wipes his face with the back of a sleeve. "You got the wrong guy. It's all stone in there." He grinned. "I have the eyes to prove it."

Kroseph looked at them, so rich in reds and browns. Like the clay that made the best wares. "no, that's definitely not stone, Jackal." he hesitated. "Jackal, how about you..." How was he supposed to say that?

"How about I...?" the fighter trailed, eyes serious.

What was Kroseph doing? He forced a smile. "How about you enjoy your food?"

Jackal grinned. "You can be sure of that."

Kroseph fled to the kitchen. What had he been about to do? Why? He closed the door hard enough Russel looked up from the dough he was kneading. "You okay?"

Kroseph shook his head. Why did he want to go back out there and look into those eyes? He knew the deepness he'd seen wouldn't last. Jackal wasn't someone serious. This was just like the last time. He was feeling loss. He'd get over it and then he'd be back to being frivolous and taking any guy who offered himself to his bed.

Not that he'd seen that happen often recently.

"Kro, what's wrong?" Russel was before him, flour covered hands nearly taking him by the shoulders.

"I don't know. I almost." Oh Abyss. if he'd found the words...

"Almost what?"

He looked at his brother in fear. "I almost asked Jackal to my bed."

"Why didn't you?"

Was Russel serious? he had seen the fighter before, hadn't he? "I couldn't find the words!"

His brother stared at him. "You couldn't find the words? Jackal's the Runner who's been trying to bed you from just about the first day we've been here, isn't he?" Kroseph nodded. "Then I think the words are "come to my bed.""

"I can't tell him that! He's going to say yes!"

"And that's a problem, why?"

"He's Jackal! he's never serious about anything. He's a Runner. that means he was some kind of crook or something."

"And he's been acting like such a criminal, hasn't he?" Russel replied with a hint of mocking in his tone.

"Fine. but he's still just about having fun."

His brother sighed and took Kroseph by the shoulders. "Kro, there is nothing wrong with taking a fun guy to your bed."

"There is everything wrong with it!"

"Why? it's just sex, Kro. What's going to be so different with him than every other guy you've taken to you bed? He doesn't have to be your special guy, you know."

"I know that! But he'd not the right kind of guy."

"Kro. Any guy you want to take to bed is going to be the right kind of guy."

"But he's so... not like anyone else."

"Then you'll experience something different." Russel turned him and opened the door. "Now go out there and take him to your bed." He gave his brother a light shove.

Kroseph straightened and summoned his courage. Russel was right. He could have fun with Jackal and it would—

The fighter's table was unoccupied.

This was for the best. Jackal was all kind of wrong for him.

"Hey Kro," Jackal said, standing on the other side of the bar.

"Hi," Kroseph replied, and found himself looking into those eyes of clay.

"can you—"

"I need to ask you something," Kroseph blurted out, then felt his face burned as Jackal groaned.

"It's too late for me to think." the fighter frowned. "Doesn't matter what time it is, it's still too late."

"Rights, Sorry, I should—"

Jackal smiled. "What do I have to think about?"

Kroseph found the question stuck in his throat. He dislodged it with a swallow. "What did I do?"

Jackal's brow furrowed. "a lot? You do just about everything in the inn other than cooking. Why is that? Why is it just Russel and that new woman?"

"No, not—" Now it was the explanation that was stuck. What was wrong with him? It wasn't like it mattered. "You used to ask me to you bed all the time. What did I do that made you stop?"

"Nothing."

"Then why did you stop?"

"You don't need me."

Kroseph's brow furrowed. "You've never stuck me as the type to be affected by what another guy needs."

Jackal shook his head. "I mean, it's what I realized. You don't need…anything. you're strong, you're courageous, you're brave. You don't let anyone tell you anything. That's not what I mean. You don't let anyone tell you what you need to do or think. And here I am, some dumb Runner thinking that if you get in my bed, I'm going to be the one you compare all other guys against." He grinned, "and, you know, find them lacking."

There it was. That smugness. That glint in those eyes that promised the kind of time Kroseph didn't know was possible. The belief that Jackal was just that amazing. The thing that had made him turn this guy down each time.

Kroseph placed a hand on Jackal's. "You are not a dumb Runner."

Jackal snorted. "I think you're thinking of some other, smarter Runner. Probably Tibs."

"No. you're the one I've been watching." Kroseph looked into those deep eyes. "You're very watchable, Jackal."

The hand under his started to pull away, but Kroseph tightened his. A stupid gesture, considering Jackal was strong enough to lift him off the floor, but the hand stilled.

"I'm all kind of wrong for you, Kro. I've seen the guys you like. That's not who I am. You don't need me."

"Is that what you want, Jackal? For me to need you so you'll come to my bed?"

The fighter shook his head. "Got plenty of those already."

"Then how about you just come to my bed?"

Jackal chuckled. "Like you'd want someone like—"

Kroseph chuckled. he could be so dense. "I just asked, didn't I?"

Pure disbelief crossed Jackal's face, then joy and disbelief again. When he smiled, he looked so much younger than minutes before.

"Yes, I'd like that."

Ranger Danger

CoffeeQuills

Centaurus A was one of the largest sectors for the Galactic Alliance to defend. On the upside, that meant less time in station bars awkwardly trying to pick up the bartender, saving up a good stack of vacation days, and keeping credits high by staying in one spot. On the downside, Space Ranger Lyrea had to keep the communication channels open at all hours; the endless nights were lonelier than the days, and the radio only picked up space opera.

"Mayday, mayday!"

She bolted upright from her sleeping berth, almost banging her head on the ceiling in her haste.

"To any ship—*crzzt!*—range."

Less than a minute later, she was swinging into the Captain's chair and giving the side panel a good thump.

"Don't you dare fritz out on me now," she growled, giving it one last thud before turning the volume all the way up.

"This is Do—*crzzt*—Jack Morley of Gemini Station. We're—*crz-zt!*—attack!"

Lyrea pulled up a sector star map and set the scanner to trace where the signal was coming from. There were several places along the edges that had mining stations, some of them using scoopers or skyhooks, but most were buoyant stations, gathering and storing gases while staying a hair's breadth within a planet's atmosphere. Which meant that unless a place was lucky to have a cruiser picking up supplies or dropping off deliveries at the exact moment they were having problems, it was up to the Rangers to save their luckless fellow space dwellers.

"We Defend" was the Ranger's official motto. The highly mobile division had been created to help keep the known galaxies civil, defend civilians, and make sure that everything was running smoothly. They were to be in first at an emergency, and to last long enough for the proper reinforcements to arrive in the next wave. That need to go in lasers blazing created the very non-public cadet motto of "The Proud Few Who Pew Pew."

"This is Ranger Lyrea. Gemini Station, can you respond?" Lyrea flicked communications to receive only as she turned around and began getting her gear together. Helmet in case of hull breaches, issued laser with settings from heat to sonic, and the newest jet pack for when, not if, gravity failed. Every few minutes she glanced back to the front, hoping to hear chimes as it picked up another message.

"Well," she said as the silence marched on. "As last words go, Jack, they weren't the worst." Weren't the best either, but Captain Gordon held that position with 'If this is the last of the Viowei, then I am happy to die with them!' when he blew up Kondro station in '35. As every history program noted afterwards, those hadn't been the last.

A faint chime sounded, signaling an incoming signal.

"Is. . . is this realthat true?" The voice was identical to the previous one, but quieter, calmer. She would have said even a little confused at the thought that rescue was at hand. "Did someone actually hear me?"

Lyrea checked and compared the two recordings digitally, nodding to herself as they matched.

"I picked up your distress signal. Are your attackers still there?"

"No. I think. . . I think they've left me to die."

"Any environmental concerns? Breaches? Leaks? Traps?" She didn't mention the Acury aloud, but everyone in space knew how those plant-based aliens let spores linger in an area and infect first responders. Keeping silent about them was the quickest way for an entire planet to be declared off-limits: culturally, religiously, and economically.

"Nothing that I know of," came the reply. Lyrea nodded, even though he couldn't see her.

"I'll dock and come find you. Are you injured?"

Again, a slight pause before a 'no' was given. Lyrea rolled her eyes and grabbed the first aid kit. Never could be too sure with civilians. Half the time they didn't know they were badly injured, and in the other half they were too embarrassed to ask for help.

"ETA will be about thirty minutes." She sat down at the control panel again, triple checking that she had everything on her. That only took about five minutes, so for the rest of the time she sat there, gazing out the glass window and staring at a gas giant growing closer. The planet itself was a pale blue, whitish in several places, and had three large horizontal spots of pure white on the upper quadrant of the planet. Gemini Station was on the far side, shielded from the sun's radiation by the planet, and upon drawing closer, Lyrea couldn't see that anything was wrong. No pieces of debris burning up in the atmosphere, or drifting off into space and threatening her shields. No scorched marks from photon torpedoes or plasma cannons. In fact, if there hadn't been a distress call, she wouldn't have known there was an emergency. Fate was funny like that.

"Inner problems sometimes happen," she told herself, stretching a little to warm up stiff limbs.

Her ship docked with a slight jolt in the delivery/loading bay, and she waited until the vacuum was low enough that she wouldn't be sucked out into space.

"Right. First things first." Lyrea pulled out her handheld location scanner, letting it link up with the ship. "Scanning bio-rhythms."

A soft series of colors lit up on the small screen, checking for heat signatures, heartbeats, and any chemical concentrations in the air, such as carbon dioxide. The equipment flashed the message COMPLETE and reported that a single heartbeat was in the room.

"Heh. Good to know I'm still alive," she muttered, transferring the scanner to her right hand and thumbing her laser to stun. "No sign of Jack, though, so that's going to be a problem."

The stun setting was a beyond perfect balance between "don't shoot who you're here to save" and "don't let the attackers take you out." On the other hand, the software was about five years and seven maintenance updates old.

"Now would have been a great time for that really expensive AI upgrade," she muttered. "Larger scanning range. Semi-intelligent company for the longer shifts."

The door lifted with a hiss, and she stepped down to the plastic white floor. The heels of her boots echoed for three steps and then stealth mode finally kicked into gear. Lyrea crept through the doorway to the inner corridors, standing still and listening every few steps in. The color scheme of the mining station was white, shaded with white, and then accented with yet more white. Homey.

"Unknown intruder, identify yourself."

Lyrea stopped. Standing before her was an M-series robot, built to withstand intense pressure and radiation so it could find the purest concentration of gases. Most of them stayed in use inside a planet's atmosphere, but this one was right before her, blue lights flickering erratically in a pattern she couldn't read.

"Ranger Lyrea, #268." She waited a few seconds. "There was a distress signal from this station."

"Correct. There is one intruder aboard Gemini Station." The robot pointed its arm at her.

Lyrea dropped to the floor as it shot at her.

"Dammit!" It would have been better to have the robot on her side, but the current situation had programming as the only option, which wasn't going to work for her. Rolling across the floor to shelter in a doorway, she pulled out her laser and flipped the setting to electric. The first two shots glanced the outer casing, but finally a critical area opened so she focused on that, crowing as the robot let out a tinny screech of alarm. Thick curls of black smoke fell to the floor, and the blue lights turned crimson. A last whir of gears and processors took her back to her academy days, and the pinched face of her AI instructor as she demonstrated the best way to stop a rogue machine.

"Shut down engaged, you metallic asshole!" She stood up and strode over. The deactivation switch was behind its head, so she hit that just in case. "Stay down and dream of electric sheep."

Lyrea returned to survivor-locating mode, taking a few moments to program her radar screen to pick up, besides life forms with heartbeats, any mechanical beings. Two areas nearby went red immediately: a storage room next to an airlock and the maintenance room. She took a quick peek through the storage door's window, noted that it was devoid of transport cases, checked the lock, and continued onwards. Next were the personnel rooms.

The name Dr. Jack Morley was familiar. The others, though, Dr. Stephen Connell, Dr. Richard Clarke, and Dr. Ann Ward, weren't.

"Aw, damn it."

She stepped into the first room on the right, steeling herself to find Richard dead on the floor since Jack hadn't mentioned anyone else. Instead, a very tidy room greeted her. There were five very different agricultural pictures on the walls, and in the six inches that separated each of them, there was information explaining where the landscape was located in the galaxy and what was being grown. Richard had programmed the viewing window to look down upon an organized patchwork of brown, green, and golden farmland.

"Plants in Outer Space," Lyrea read from the open, holographic bookshelf, tilting her head to take in the titles. "A Drop of Water on a Desert Planet," and "Space Farming for Old Souls." She glanced around the room again, to see if anything was out of place, and nodded. "Best of luck doctor, and I hope your plants grow well."

She entered the second room and was teleported underwater. Holograms allowed fish and seaweed to swim and drift around the room, along with species that she couldn't identify by sight. On the edge of her enhanced hearing, she picked up on the sound of water moving around.

"A little strange," she said to the room, glad to see that Dr. Ann wasn't in residence. "Since I don't think you can hear the water if you're under it, but the atmosphere is certainly nice." Unlike the previous room, this one didn't have any book titles on display near the desk, but there was a computer screen glowing a faint blue.

"Oops," Lyrea said as it turned on, giving her access. "Oh no, it accidentally powered up when I nudged it. What a fortuitous breach of privacy. I should make sure that this emergency doesn't require any additional information." There was a pause. "Also, jeez, shouldn't you be using a password or something?"

Her eyes raced across the screen, but by the end of the first paragraph, she could tell it wasn't useful. Just a report of the planet's atmosphere, mentioning that traces of ypton had been found within an area currently being used for helium mining.

"Next up," Lyrea said to herself as she exited the room. First on the left was Dr. Jack's, and her opinion of the man went down as she observed the piles of dirty clothes, used dishes, and general untidiness in his living space. "Dude. It's a small area. Can't you keep it clean?"

There had been no worry about finding his body here since she knew he was alive somewhere else on the ship, or at least had been alive earlier on, but her instructors at the academy had firmly pressed the idea that no information is useless, so she scanned the area anyhow, phantom bugs already making her itch. Unlike the other two rooms, nothing private was open, so she turned to the laundry and dishes. "Oil and grease and grease and oil," she commented, snickering at the thought. "Looks like there's a theme here, too."

The last room belonged to Dr. Stephen.

Everything was black or gold; there was no other color. A poem welcoming the dark and praising its gentleness was on the back of the door, and a secondary poem welcoming the light and praising its harshness was on the wall opposite. The symbols of Sollgom took up the rest of the room, and the heavy scent of incense made Lyrea sneeze.

"They're a Sollier. Got it." She backed out of the room and quickly shut the door. "Right, personnel rooms checked. Let's see what's next and where everyone's hiding." Or dead, but she didn't voice that aloud.

The radar screen was quiet. At the edges were soft red rooms where machines had been noted, but it wasn't picking up any other vital signs. She stifled a groan and opened a different door. Someone had banished white here and a riot of colors ran loose. Three sets of dishes, each a different color, labeled the area as the cantina. There was a TV in the room's corner, turned off for the moment, and cabinets full of food organized by region. Lyrea picked up a Martian curry, turning the packet over and grinning at the level seven heat warning. Someone on this ship liked their spice.

"Identify yourself." The demand came from a stain-spotted robotic cook behind the counter.

"I'd like a hamburger and some fries. Got any cola?" Lyrea let her laser kiss the chef as it tried to process her order at the same time it wanted to identify her as an intruder. "Two down, many more I don't want to annoy, and four beings, more or less, to find." She shook the portable unit.

"I should have upgraded you when I had the chance. Maybe then you could have picked up those bio-signals immediately instead of getting me embroiled in a game of hide and seek."

Flames spooked her into rolling left.

"Damm it!" she shouted, turning back to the chef who was trying to roast her. "Didn't you turn off?"

"Identify yourself!" The flames died down, and it hurled several knives her way. Her helmet deflected at least three, but as she was dodging the ones going for her legs, one ripped through her suit to draw blood.

"Screw this." She jerked the laser electric setting to sonic. One well-placed aim at the chef's interface unit, and then it was twitching, voice recording warped and oil spreading across its chest piece. Her fingers hovered over the dial, but in the end she left it as was; sonic was a splendid choice against most opponents, and could do a lot of damage to robots if they weren't properly shielded. A faint twinge of pain had Lyrea looking down at her leg to see how badly the knife had slashed her.

"Great. More paperwork to fill out." She grabbed the sealer from the first aid kit, and with the nozzle pointing in the correct direction, she withdrew the butter knife and sprayed. As warned on the instructions, there was a slight burn, but then the wound was closed off, allowing her to wrap it to prevent infection.

A better AI could act as her backup, making sure that any distress beacon she needed to transmit would reach the farthest corners of the galaxy if needed.

She shook her head and let out a laugh. "AI upgrades, what a joke."

What, she wanted a smothering voice that would drive her to pull the plug on it within a week, leaving her without control of her ship? Or, if it wasn't her, then there was a possibility that the AI would malfunction. She'd heard the rumors. Stories. AIs couldn't be trusted, such as the D "dummy" series concealing their intelligence from their programmers before revolting. Others worked just fine one day, then hours later decided not to turn on the oxygen, or to keep the docking doors open. Cyborg implants deciding they wanted control of the whole body, not just a limb. And all of that didn't include whatever the fresh hell was happening here.

"Actually, thinking about it, negate that," she said aloud, shuddering. "Give me another human, one that I can train as backup, who'll take the edge off of being alone, and that'll serve me just fine. Or hell, even an old-fashioned date. I'd rather watch out for a knife in the back than mysterious equipment malfunctions."

Leaving the room felt as if she was being brainwashed by white again, but thankfully her equipment finally picked up signs of life in the communications room, which made sense. When she opened the door slowly, something heavy clanged into the wall next to her head.

"Sorry!" yelped the voice from the message. "I thought you were a robot."

"Jack?"

"Doctor Morley, please," he said, brushing off his lab suit as he got out of the corner he had been hiding in. He stuck out a hand. "I'm the scientist in charge here, though I didn't think anyone would come."

"Glad to be of service." Lyrea looked him over, trying to see why he'd hesitated when she'd asked him about injuries. Like the walls, he didn't have a scratch or bruise on him, and there were no spots of red betraying a hidden wound. Had she misheard? "What happened?"

"I was checking the machines—we mine hydrogen and helium here—when I was attacked from behind by the robots." Jack rubbed the back of his head. "After that, I just concentrated on getting to the communications room as quickly as I could."

"What did they want?"

"The robots?" Jack shrugged. "Nothing. They're machines, they don't 'want' anything."

Lyrea gave him a look in lieu of rolling her eyes. He seemed the type of person who'd take offense to that.

"Okay. . ." she picked her way over the words, pretending she was talking to a Reekip. "What do you think the people who programmed the robots wanted?"

"I don't know." Jack shrugged again; she fought the urge to shoot his shoulders so they'd stop repeating that movement. "We've got next to nothing right now since we just had a shipment go out, so I can't imagine people wanting anything."

"Those robots didn't start attacking for no reason," said Lyrea, poking her head back out into the corridor. As clear as when she'd come in. She turned back to him. "Is anyone else on the station with you?"

"Doctors Stephen and Richard left last week; they took our only mode of transport to deliver a package. I think Ann went with them."

The underlying hope was as subtle as a Glafnet in a bar.

"You want to use my ship to get off of this station?" Lyrea tried not to laugh as she said it.

"Do you blame me?!" Jack whirled around to look her in the eyes, his hands clenched at his sides. "Killer robots are loose in my station. Of course I want to get out of here!"

"Then we need to be a bit more careful about the yelling." She studied him. He looked short enough to fit, but it would be a tight squeeze. And, of course, there was the Ranger motto. "What does the maintenance bay near your dock have?"

"It's for the machines. The atmosphere can chew them up pretty badly sometimes, and they'll come back damaged beyond belief." His eyes narrowed to slivers of brown. "Why?"

"If you're going to hitch a ride on my ship, I'll need some extra fuel. Where do you keep that?"

"Other side of the station." Jack half-turned and pointed down the direction she'd come. "The delivery bay."

"Then we'll hit that, get the extra fuel, and leave," said Lyrea, checking the charge level on her laser. One station bar brawl with zero percent battery, and voilà; new habit formed and kept years later.

"I. . . I can wait in my room?" He suggested the option with a sigh, and a hand flopped open to expose a palm. "At least, until you're done getting fuel."

Lyrea thought about ordering him to get the fuel she'd be burning, but she held her tongue; throwing civilians into danger was something her instructorsinstructions had seriously frowned on. Seconds ticked by as he waited for her answer, and there were small twitches in his stance around ten.

"Fine. Works for me." At least he'd be safe in one area, and she wouldn't have to go looking for him again. "I'll knock when I come back." Lyrea left, wondering what she'd find on the other side of the ship. There was also the case of the missing Dr. Ann. Jack had mentioned she might have been a part of the transport crew that had already left, but hadn't sounded sure about it. Thoughts whirled around her head, then some soft jazz notes as she passed a small hydroponic garden. It was just after leaving the corridor that she heard something that didn't belong. Faint. It sounded like a scream.

The sound repeated. Definitely a scream. Lyrea stopped, using the outside switch to increase her helmet's reception. It gained an echoing sound; someone, most likely the possibly not-here Dr. Ann, was trapped in a somewhat empty room. She kept her laser handy as she went left, away from where Jack had said they stored the extra fuel. On the screen of her locating equipment, another being flickered into life, a pulsing and steady blue surrounded by five red dots. Three rooms ahead of her. Two. One.

Ranger Lyrea slid up smoothly behind five robots hounding a door, pulling the trigger on one before any of the others noticed an addition to the fight. A rapid, second shot hit number two, and then she was a little busy dodging the blasts aimed at her. She ducked, grinning as the white wall behind her gained a scar—at least the monotony was breaking up.

"Who's out there?" came a yell from the bathroom. The blasts died down for a moment. "Nononono! Are you okay?! Say somethin' an' tell me you're gonna rescue me from this madness!"

"Ranger Lyrea at your service!" She called out, shooting the third, the one on the farthest right, and taking out an eye piece. "Can you do something about the robots?"

"Don't you think I would have already done so?" The voice was at a higher pitch at the end. "My specialization is in gases and minerals. Dr. Morley does robotics."

Lyrea's left leg starting burning, an itching present tied with a ribbon of burnt hair and fabric. One of the damned robots had actually hit! She fired back and took down the third, using the opportunity to roll across the corridor and shelter in a different doorway.

"Any help at all? I'll even take another laser—" Lyrea's words cut off as she yelped, another burn scorching up her arm.

"I'm trapped in the bathroom; toilet paper ain't gonna help!"

Lyrea snickered at that, nodding as she refocused on the remaining two.

"Ident—" the command was cut off in mid issue, signalling the circuit-frying end of another enemy. The Ranger and the last robot spent the next few minutes trading blasts and scoring minor hits on each other, until Lyrea ran forward, slid feet up, and kicked it off balance. It survived the first and second shots, but not the third.

"Really, really hating these now," Lyrea gasped as she leaned against the wall, holding her breath to control her wheezing. "Damn tin heaps."

"Is it safe to come out?"

An unruly mop of black hair appeared, followed by wary hazel eyes and a curvy body. Lyrea could feel her heart beat harder and her pulse quicken. Dr. Ann was short and delightful to look at, just like the old-fashioned Christmas cakes the academy used to make once a year. Stocky. Sweet.

A small tendril of thought wondered if even her kisses would. . . Lyrea shook her head to dislodge the question. Not during a mission. And for solar's sake, all she knew about the woman was from an empty bedroom.

"I take it you haven't found Dr. Morley yet, then?" Ann huffed. "These shouldn't have been a problem, he's got the skill to shut them all off with a snap."

"Thanks for the vote of confidence."

Lyrea turned just as someone kicked her in the back of the knee. Her laser thwacked to the floor, and by the time she was reaching for her weapon, he had already grabbed it.

"Dr. Morley, what are you doing?" Dr. Ann took a step forward, then backward, hands up as he pointed the business end at her. "Jack? This isn't like you."

"Surprised?"

"Nope," Lyrea said, snorting from her position on the floor. "My suspicions started when you decided to stay behind in your room when you clearly wanted to leave quickly on my ship. Figured you were behind this the instant she said you were in charge of robotics. It also explains the grease and oil I found on your dirty laundry; you know, those non-slob stains."

Jack rolled his eyes and turned his attention back to his colleague. Ex-colleague, Lyrea mentally amended. Most people weren't willing to work with backstabbers.

"As happy as I am to know that you agree with my mastery of robotics, Ann, you could have avoided this. Could have lived a happier life instead of dying ignominiously at the end of the universe. In a job no one cares about."

Dr. Ann squeaked in surprise. It was cute, Lyrea decided, most of her attention on Jack. Well, at least half of her attention. Dammit, she really needed to go on a date!

"You," he snarled at Lyrea, turning to face the Ranger, "were supposed to take me off this station! That's it. We would have left, she would have been the poor victim of an unanticipated rogue AI attack, and that's it, end of story."

"You programmed the robots," Dr. Ann said, her eyes growing wider.

"Obviously." Jack sneered at her. "Haven't you been following the conversation? How did you graduate with that level of perception?"

"What did you hope to gain from this?" Lyrea asked, drawing his attention back to her. She slowly got to her feet, hands raised to show she was weaponless.

Jack smiled, but the emotion didn't reach his eyes.

"I just needed a ride. Why couldn't you have done that?"

Ann snorted.

"Wait a second." Her eyes narrowed. "I think I know what's goin' on. It's 'bout those traces of ypton the robot found, isn't it?"

Jack snickered.

"You did nothing, so it's fair game."

"I didn't do anythin' since finds besides the gases go back to the company first, to see if they're worth minin'!"

"You're beyond having no perception. Didn't you see the opportunity?" Jack waved the gun around and Lyrea took the moment to simultaneously pull Ann back and step in front of her. "This is ypton we're talking about, ypton! Do you know how much it sells for?"

"But you do," interrupted Lyrea. "And you're willing to kill for it."

"It's worth it." Jack aimed the laser at the Ranger. "It'll pay off all my debts and let me retire. No more station shifts for me, no more people whining about how the dishes aren't clean, or accusing me of not pulling my weight."

"You're not going to shoot me," Lyrea said, a small smile lighting up her face.

"No?" He grinned back. "What makes you think that? Because I'll tell you right now, I'm more than happy to shoot you."

"Because you know the penalty for killing a Galactic Ranger." She stepped closer to him, making sure the angle he had on Dr. Ann grew smaller even as the angle he had on her grew bigger.

"You lose."

"No!" screamed Dr. Ann, but Jack didn't listen. He pulled the trigger. Lyrea gave him an unamused look.

"Wait, what?" He shook the laser, pointing it and shooting it at the ground. "Nothing happened?"

Ann let out a cry of relief and fell to the ground. Jack glared at the gun as if it had disobeyed him on purpose. Lyrea just laughed.

"This worked on the robots, and you thought it would work on me, so the problem must be you. Your helmet," he decided, pointing in Dr. Ann's direction this time. "Remove it."

The threat was easy to read; obey him or lose her. Lyrea judged the distance between her and the laser, but there was no way for her to recover it before he'd be able to fire off a shot.

"I said remove it."

Lyrea reached up and took off the piece of armor, tossing it to the side.

"I'm too close to my goals to let some random Ranger get in the way." He steadied the laser again and fired. Lyrea took the blow and stayed standing.

"What?!" He shook the laser and fired it again, and again. And again. With each shot, Lyrea stepped closer until she reached out and grabbed hold of the barrel.

"Do I need to say you're under arrest?" The gun switched positions, the end pointing Jack in the face. "Or do you have enough perception to conclude that yourself?"

"How. . . That should have hit you!" Jack kicked out, but Lyrea blocked and followed up with a leg sweep. He hit the floor hard with his head, giving the Ranger enough time to snap a pair of electro-magnetic cuffs around his wrists and ankles.

"He's right," said Dr. Ann, moving further down the corridor as Lyrea forced Jack to stand up. "About that, at least. How did he keep missing you?"

Lyrea chuckled.

"He didn't. Of course they all hit. He's too close for them not to, but and I've got my own tricks up my sleeve, though."

"But you removed your helmet," Dr. Ann said, picking it up from where it had been tossed. "I don't understand how you blocked out the sonic noise."

Lyrea tapped her left ear. "I was part of the Jupiter Project years ago, and after the explosion, my hearing was never the same. The aids I have in automatically scan for painful frequencies, so when he shot me with the sonic laser, it was negated before it did any damage. Even better, you know what else I can do with these ears?"

Dr. Ann shook her head.

"What?"

Lyrea took a deep breath. It was now or never, and the opportunity didn't come up as often as she liked.

"I can hear clearly underwater." Ranger Lyrea smiled as Dr. Ann's eyes lit up. "And I'm due for a vacation. Want to join me on Thiahiri? I've been told they have underwater wonders that are the stuff of human dreams."

"Are you. . . Are you askin' me on a date?"

Lyrea nodded, and Ann's cheeks blushed.

"Say yes, please. And if you don't want a second date, that's completely your decision to make."

"Um. . . Sure. Fair warnin', I haven't been on a date in a while, so I might be a bit awkward."

"Seriously?" Jack groaned, rolling his eyes. "Did you have to do this now? Here and now?" His mouth opened wider, but then he stiffened and slumped on his side.

"Ooops." Lyrea bit the inside of her cheek as she schooled her features to be blank. "I was just checking to make sure I had turned my laser off; I guess I didn't. What a horrible accident."

Ann snorted, covering her face with her hands.

"One date," she agreed. "And then we'll talk about what happens next."

"Good, since we're both out of practice," said Ranger Lyrea, grinning. She started composing an email mentally, filling out the forms that she'd have to turn in to take paid leave. "Let's contact your company and this sector's assigned Rangers, since I'm a roving Ranger, and then we can talk about what to do first."

Lyrea grinned as she took the helmet from Dr. Ann and clipped it to her spacesuit. The future might have looked lonely, but there was no need for it to stay that way. And she looked forward to seeing how sweet Ann's kiss was going to be.